At first I didn't see it. There was, after all, a sofa blocking the view. Miranda Travers lay, body twisted but faceup, one arm flung out wide. She was wearing a long ivory silk nightdress and a matching negligee trimmed with lace. Very good lace. A small satin-and-swansdown mule lay on its side near one bare foot. She looked like Ophelia: fragile, pathetic. But there were no flowers. The index fingers of the outstretched hand seemed to be pointing directly at my book, lying facedown where I had left it by the armchair. I picked it up. The word *Murder* in the title leapt out at me.

MURDER
UNDER THE
MISTLETOE

JENNIFER JORDAN

WORLDWIDE.

TORONTO • NEW YORK • LONDON
AMSTERDAM • PARIS • SYDNEY • HAMBURG
STOCKHOLM • ATHENS • TOKYO • MILAN
MADRID • WARSAW • BUDAPEST • AUCKLAND

To my father, in loving memory

MURDER UNDER THE MISTLETOE

A Worldwide Mystery/December 1998

First published by St. Martin's Press, Incorporated.

ISBN 0-373-26295-7

MURDER
UNDER THE
MISTLETOE

ONE

Dee

IT ALL STARTED in Spring. In Italy—Florence, to be precise. To be even more precise, in front of the aptly entitled Botticelli painting, *La Primavera*, in the Uffizi Gallery. I'd been to Italy before—to Venice (where it rained solidly for most of the holiday, but was marvellous on the three fine days we did have), and, many, many moons ago, as a sort of au pair-cum-companion-cum-English tutor. After the first week, when everyone, including myself, was bewildered by my exact status, or lack of it (was I a servant, a Bronte-ish governess, a guest, or what?), I cabled home a request for funds and became a paying-guest-cum-companion-cum-English tutor. Which meant I still mucked in with the washing-up, but out of goodwill, and my lessons with Flavia, who was only two years younger than I was, anyway, were pared down to an hour a day—no sweat, because she was pretty good and bound to waltz through the Cambridge Certificate with no trouble. So, I had a wonderful time with Flavia and her crowd, especially when everyone departed *en masse* for the coast for the summer season. And the tricky question of my status was settled. Europeans are even more status-conscious than the Brits— well, look at the way the Italians address everyone as 'Ingegnere' and 'Professore' and so on. A common or garden infant teacher of twenty-one is entitled to the swish title of 'Professoressa'—as is my husband, Barry, who is a fully paid-up member of the NUT and a lecturer in History at Woodfield Technical College, Outer London.

Anyway, I had spent a short time in Florence with Flavia and her family, before we departed to the delights of Positano, but that, as I have indicated, was in the dim and distant past, and Florence is the kind of timeless place to which one always wants to return. So, when Barry suggested we should spend the Easter vacation abroad, I suggested we should stay in Florence and soak up the art and culture, driving to any accessible Italian towns that took our fancy. We picked up an Alfa Giulietta from a car-hire firm in Rome, and after a couple of days exploring the Colosseum et al, motored to Florence and anchored ourselves at a hotel along the Lungarno, which proved horrendously expensive but was modern and ultra-comfortable. It had been Flavia's suggestion, so, come to think of it, no wonder the prices were a bit gasp-making. However, we could afford it, for once—Barry, who writes humorous crime novels on the side, had secured a lucrative contract for a second television series, the first (*Penny For The Guy, Dead On Time,* etc) having been positively lapped up by the viewers.

Flavia is impoverished nobility on her father's side—which means a dark and gloomy palazzo within walking distance of Piazza Santa Croce, and plutocratic industrialism on her mother's—which means the palazzo is furnished in opulent comfort and there's a flat in Milan and the villa at Positano as well. Now that she's married to Luigi and has produced one of the 2.2 requisite bambini, she drives in from Settignano twice a week, leaving little Paolo to the care of his part-time nanny, Teresa, and does her stint at a very chic boutique in Via dei Calzaoli. I phoned Flavia the evening we arrived in la bella Firenze, and emerged from the cascade of *ciao, carissima*'s and *tanto, tanto piacere*'s, having accepted an invitation to dinner at their villa, once we had had time to do some sightseeing.

We were surprisingly lucky with the weather, the sky remaining a clear della Robbia blue, unusual for April, though there was the occasional sharpish breeze and little wavelets scudded now and then along the yellowish Arno. As I had predicted, Barry rapidly fell under the spell of this unique and ancient city, home of the medieval guilds of craftsmen, of the Medici banking family, and of the awful Savonarola. With him I shopped for leather goods in the open market, looked at the San Marco frescoes and had a romantic evening meal in the Piazzale Michelangelo, overlooking the city. The Ghiberti doors of the Duomo needed attention, but everything else was fine, just fine.

I SUPPOSE the Uffizi Gallery is to Florence what the Louvre is to Paris. Originally intended as offices by Cosimo—hence the name—it houses one of the most magnificent collections of paintings in the world. There isn't any equivalent to the *Mona Lisa,* but the Botticellis are the nearest bet. Everyone wants to see them, anyway—including us. Barry had his horn-rimmed specs on—the ones he wears when he's typing out his masterpieces; or wading through some tome about the Thirty Years War or the Chartists; or trying to impress students with his erudition, or his earnestness, or something. He had that slightly glazed look, horn-rims notwithstanding, which comes after exposure to several rooms of saints and madonnas and golden backgrounds. Giotto and his followers can be pretty overpowering *en masse.*

He cheered up when we came to the works of Sandro Filipepi, alias Botticelli. I dug him in the ribs, and murmured, 'You ain't seen nothin' yet, kid.' Which, in a sense, he hadn't. After all, we had the rest of the Uffizi to go through, and then the

Pitti, and the Bargello and the Accademia, not to mention a couple of assorted palaces with artistic goodies. Not all on the same day, of course. Luckily we had the time to be cultural gourmets. I've always felt sorry for those parties who are whizzed through places like the Uffizi and emerge an hour later, ready for their next port of call, but suffering from visual indigestion and severe frustration.

Barry enjoyed the Botticellis so much that we went round them a second time, having decided that we'd go off for some refreshment before tackling the rest of the gallery. Which I'd seen, of course, in the dim and distant, but Barry hadn't. It was on our second trip round that we saw The Girl. Or The Vision, which, to judge by Barry's expression, is what he thought she was. She was standing in front of the *Allegory of Spring* (or *Primavera*) canvas—a tallish, slender (but not too slender) figure wearing a long floaty dress in white, sprigged with little green bunches of flowers. The kind of dress which wasn't in fashion that year, but the way she wore it somehow one got the feeling it was, or at any rate that it soon would be.

She had long, floaty hair, too—various little loops casually arranged about her head, and the rest of the mane flowing straight down her back, almost to the waist. It was that indefinable colour between golden-brown and blonde, with a tinge of sherry. So that you couldn't exactly call her a blonde, but

it was difficult to think of an alternative, as she
certainly wasn't a brunette either. The get-up
seemed calculated, but perhaps it wasn't. When she
turned and moved on the similarity was striking.
She might have been Botticelli's favourite Simo-
netta Vespucci, or one of her kin, moved into the
nineteen eighties. The face was a long oval, with a
faintly cleft chin, the nose straight and delicate, the
neck long, and the mouth sweetly curved, with a
full lower lip. Since she was looking down at her
museum guide I didn't see what colour her eyes
were, but Barry assured me afterwards that they
were blue. He gave an appreciative wolf-whistle
under his breath as The Vision wafted on, and indicated the girl on the left-hand side of *La Primavera*—the one who seems to be taking part in a
dance based on Ring o' Roses, with two others.
Apart from the fact that she was garbed in diaphanous, swirling draperies and The Vision was wearing sprigged cotton (however Botticellian the style)
certainly she could have been a dead ringer for The
Vision. Or vice-versa.

'Cor!' Barry murmured. 'Italian girls certainly
have something.'

'She's British.' My tone was brisk, if not sharp.
My better half loves me dearly, as I do him, but
he's by no means immune to other feminine
charms. Like Louise Larousse, late of the Woodfield Tech, currently of the Faubourg something-or-

other in Paris, where she cooks and irons for one Jean-Pierre, whom she married with much fanfare of trumpets last month.

'Oh.' Barry digested this information for a moment, before following it up with the obvious, 'How do you know?'

'Her guide's written in English. Of course, she could be American.' (Or Australian, Canadian, or some other nationality which has English as its second language and doesn't read guide books in French, Italian or German).

'Oh.' Barry was now gazing at *La Primavera* again, but my attention had been caught by a man standing a few feet away from The Vision. He was even more incredible than she was, in a completely different way, being dressed completely in black— black trousers tucked into calf-length boots, black shirt striped in charcoal grey, a flowing black cloak, and, to complete the ensemble, a black floppy felt hat. He had strongly marked features, a beak of a nose, and black shoulder-length hair with a few threads of grey. If the girl could have been an original Botticelli maiden, he could have been a pre-Raphaelite artist—except that somehow he reminded me more of Olivier playing Richard III, without the hump.

He was staring very fixedly at The Vision, and when she drifted unhurriedly through the door into the next room, he followed. So did we, a few minutes later, but obviously they had both moved on ahead of us, as there was no sign of either of them.

After a couple more rooms of famous paintings we were both feeling like taking the load off our feet and having some lunch, but we avoided the Piazza dell Signoria, knowing that any restaurant there would be crowded—April's one of the peak tourist times in Florence, and the Uffizi is the premier port of call, after the Duomo. I suggested a little place on the other side of the river, which I remembered had done excellent rosbif alla fiorentina and lasagne al forno in the past.

'All right, Dee, you're the expert.' Barry trailed after me, having resigned himself to the fact that we'd had our last glimpse of The Vision. In this, however, he was wrong. As we emerged into the Lungarno, there she was, under the arches, examining a clutch of leather bags that were hanging up, for sale. And there, leaning against the wall of the bridge, was her cloaked and booted swain, arms folded. When she turned away from the bags and moved on, so did he.

'I say,' Barry murmured, 'do you think she's all right?'

'Anyone who looks like that is very much all right, I'd say. Dead lucky, if you ask me.'

'No, I mean that guy is obviously following her.'

'I should think she's used to that, Barry dear.

And modern girls are able to cope with that kind of thing, you know. Even in Italy.' I forbore to remark that I'd gone through the trailing routine myself, in my time, and though I've been described as 'a highly attractive redhead' and 'extremely personable' by fellows who see pretty girls every week in the course of their work, I certainly don't look like Venus on a seashell or a *Primavera* nymph.

'I suppose you're right.' Barry, bless his chivalrous little socks, sounded dubious, so just to make sure, we trailed after the cloaked and be-hatted one, but by the time we'd reached the Piazza Santa Trinita they'd both disappeared, so we crossed over the Arno and concentrated on the search for food.

Over coffee Barry expounded his idea of writing a new opus, dealing with the art and antiques world. The Uffizi, it appeared, had provided the inspiration, and now, with a nice load of pasta inside him, not to mention the famed rosbif, salad and creamy ice-cream, he was raring to get back to 'do' the other rooms. Well, after we'd had a little rest and some brandy with our next coffee.

'I thought I might call it "Framed Murder".'

'Very appropriate, darling.' I stopped myself from enquiring whether he knew enough of the art/antiques world to embark on this enterprise. After all, Barry knew very little about gourmet cooking, but that did not deter him from producing the highly successful *Proof Of The Pudding*, so far his most successful book (hardback, paperback, foreign and American sales, TV rights, two reprints). There is a hard core of determination in my husband.

ALTHOUGH I LOVE Florence and its art works, it made a nice change to drive to Settignano, where Flavia's home was perched midway up a hill, approached by a dusty lane flanked by pink and ochre houses wreathed in flowering creepers. Florence sat snugly in a basin a long way down, and even in the pallid sunshine of a rather cool Spring day, the place was picturesque and charming. It must have been delightful in summer.

Flavia kissed us both enthusiastically, and her husband greeted us warmly. Little Paolo was gorgeous—a ladykiller in the making, even as a toddler—and we sat on the terrace sipping chilled Martinis and iced limonata and swapping news. Flavia is one of the world's 'beautiful people' but she manages to be endearingly domestic as well.

Over dinner Barry described his encounters—if you could call them anything so positive—with Beauty and the Beast, as he now called them. I thought this was unfair, myself, because although the man in black certainly wouldn't rate among the world's ten most handsome men, he wasn't as ugly as that. In fact, if one went for Richard III types, he might even have been described as 'broodingly striking'.

Now, Flavia knows or knows of everybody who is anybody in Florence—and quite a few people who aren't anybody as well—so I suppose I shouldn't have been surprised when she remarked casually that she knew who both of them were. But surprised I was. Of course there's quite a British community in Florence, which has attracted the English ever since the Settecento, and although perhaps the only really celebrated British resident at the moment is Lord Acton (who hosted Prince Charles and Princess Diana when they visited Florence), there's a horde of lesser lights, right down to the art students, or researchers preparing theses on Machiavelli or Carlo Goldoni or someone. Plus, of course, the poets and sculptors and mere members of the bourgeoisie who bought dilapidated Tuscan farmhouses to renovate, in the past.

Anyway, it all goes to show that people often are, predictably, what one might guess them to be. I mean, the man, according to Flavia, was an artist, and the girl was a model. Not an artist's model, I hasten to add, but a clothes-horse model, which is marginally more respectable and infinitely better paid.

'Her name is Miranda Travers, and she is niece of old Hugh Trevor-Watkins. More wine, Barry? No? Luigi? *Bene.* This is a good wine, don't you think? It comes from our vineyards.' Luigi's family own land here and there in Italy, though he works for his livelihood in a bank. Just like the old Medici before they became rulers.

'*The* niece,' I corrected, through habit reverting to my Charlotte Bronte role. 'Should I know who old Hugh Trevor-Watkins is?' It transpired that old Hugh Trevor-Watkins—who wasn't so very old after all, a mere fifty or so—worked in some senior capacity for the British Council. And that Miranda, who had graduated at a phenomenally early age from Warwick, with a mixture of subjects, had also spent a term at Perugia University and acquired a familiarity with the language which stood her in good stead for modelling assignments with Italian magazines. I tend to classify models in categories, such as 'ethnic', 'Cockney sparrow', 'pop-art', etc. I know something about it, because before marrying Barry, and for a while after, I worked on a magazine called *Trends* and later my varied temp secretarial jobs included a stint with a fashion photographer. So it's not a new scene. The Travers girl appeared to come under the heading 'educated fringe-of-Debrett with touches of new-wave'.

The man was called Morgan Grant, and he painted small landscapes and symbolic-allegoric stuff. He was a friend of Stefano Rosselli, who sold pictures in a shop just off Piazza Goldoni, nice and central, and mounted exhibitions. Rosselli sold Grant's pictures and had exhibited him the previous year. Reaction to the exhibition had shown very modified enthusiasm, but there were occasional buyers for Grant's work. He was known to have fallen heavily for Miranda Travers, whom he met through Rosselli, and in spite of having been given the brush-off, continued to dog her footsteps—literally, it would seem. Speculation was that when Miranda left Italy, which she was due to do soon, having been booked by *Cosmopolitan*, Morgan Grant would return to his London base also.

'You're a marvel, Flavia,' Barry remarked admiringly. 'How do you know all these intimate details?'

Flavia giggled naughtily. 'First, Barry dear, I am a big gossip. And also, Luigi knows Stefano Rosselli, and he has come to dinner. So you see, it is not so difficult after all. Now, what other scandals can I tell you?'

Conversation became general over the dessert, and, our curiosity assuaged, we forgot about Morgan and Miranda.

WE WENT ON TO a few other places in the Giulietta after that evening, but when we came back, up popped Miranda Travers again, this time at a concert held in the Boboli Gardens. We went with Flavia and Luigi, and when Flavia, who was sitting on my left, jabbed her elbow into me and hissed '*Eccola!*'—or would have hissed, if the word had had any s's—naturally I didn't know who she was talking about.

'Miranda—*con lo zio.*' She jerked her head backwards, and I looked over my shoulder.

Sure enough, it was The Vision, seated beside a distinguished-looking gent with silver-grey hair in a silver-grey lightweight suit. Evidently Hugh Trevor-Watkins had acquired the Italian style of dress during his time in Florence. Miranda was in another floaty dress; it looked like white voile this time, and was sprigged with little knots of blue flowers, instead of green. The marvellous hair was brushed into a shining curtain, no loops and curls this evening, just two hairslides. The effect was of virginal simplicity, and although I didn't actually *hear* any murmurs of *'bella, bella'* from the men in her vicinity, I could *feel* the murmurs going through their minds. And, sure enough, a few rows behind there was Morgan Grant, hair still Bohemian, but cloak and hat discarded for a perfectly decent dress-suit, albeit with floppy bow-tie.

It was when I noticed the expression that had come over Miranda Travers' face that I got one of my 'funny feelings'. Barry used to ridicule these, until I'd been proved right a few times. They're sort of premonitions, really. Miranda had a satisfied little smile on her face—maybe the *'bella, bella's'* had become audible. At any rate, she knew exactly the impression she was making, and was loving every minute of it.

It suddenly struck me that Miranda Travers was a girl who might get herself into an awful lot of trouble one day. That sensational kind of beauty—sensational because it is unique—can attract every shade of feeling, from downright lust to doglike devotion, to the kind of aesthetic avarice that any work of art can induce, whether inanimate or living. And there was Morgan, looking, as Barry had said, rather like a raven—a portent of doom rather than a guardian angel.

The fact that the sky was overcast and that both the local tenor and the visiting diva chose arias from tragic operas like *Tosca,* added to my general sensation of uneasiness. The feeling was dissipated only in the interval by a diversion in the form of Stefano Rosselli, who came to pay his respects to Luigi and Flavia and was introduced to us. This resulted in an invitation to look round his shop the next day, and to lunch with him. Well, we weren't doing anything else and Barry, his mind obviously running on *Framed Murder,* accepted with alacrity. Signor Rosselli was charming, and he smiled a lot, but his eyes were sharp. I reckoned we'd be lucky to emerge without buying something, and we'd already overspent on this holiday. Oh well, as long as it wasn't a Morgan Grant original. Which was horrid of me, because for all I knew, Morgan Grant might be brilliant.

Rather to my surprise, and Barry's too, he later confessed, we both liked the Morgan Grants. The landscapes had the perfection of a modern Corot—if you can imagine that—and though the symbolic pieces seemed a bit weird, there were a couple of nice abstracts. Eventually, however, Barry chose a small impressionistic view of the Ponte Vecchio, partly because he thought I'd like it for sentimental reasons, partly because it would fit in at home, and partly because it was the second-cheapest thing on display—the cheapest was too *outré* to be considered. Stefano was obviously pleased to have made a sale—I think at one point he thought we'd escape purchaseless—and over lunch at a nearby *trattoria,* he rewarded us by giving Barry the low-down on the artistic community of Florence and its environs, plus details of what it was like to sell pictures, mount exhibitions, etc. Eventually Grant and la Travers were mentioned.

'The little Travers girl—she is very beautiful. What is it your poet John Keats says?'

'A thing of beauty is a joy forever,' Barry supplied. 'Though I think he was thinking of beautiful works of art. Non-living ones, I mean.'

'Of course. A Raphael Madonna, a Cellini bronze, Monet waterlilies, a perfect piece of china—they are all things of beauty. Really, your

Keats was very Italian. It is not surprising he chose to live in Rome.'

I refrained from pointing out that that was a matter of health, rather than choice.

'But of course, a beautiful woman is also a work of art, is it not so?' continued Rosselli. I was surprised to find that his mind was working along the same lines as mine had earlier.

'I hadn't really thought about it that way,' Barry said. To Barry, a person is a person; a fanciable girl is a fanciable girl.

'Well, I think that is partly the way Morgan sees her. He is a protégé of mine, you know, and really a talented artist. I know the way his mind works, to some extent.'

'And has he had any success with her?' Barry enquired.

Stefano Rosselli shrugged—a typically Continental gesture, which never seems quite right when British people do it. 'It depends what you mean by "success".' Barry looked embarrassed, unsure how to explain that he hadn't meant to enquire whether the gloomy-looking painter had bedded her yet.

'She keeps him on a string.' Rosselli's idiomatic English was really good, I thought, reverting to Charlotte Bronte again.

'Really, her stay here has made much embarrassment for her uncle. There have been so many men who have wanted to ask her out.' That I could believe—the Latin Romeo is anything but a myth.

'So, she goes to a concert with this one, and a film with that one, and it is all old-hat to her, because back in England she has the same thing. But I have heard the most favoured one is a Robert Thornton. He is quite rich, and handsome, too. I think she will marry him, when she is ready to marry. At the moment it is great fun not to be married for that little one.'

'Poor old Morgan Grant,' Barry remarked sympathetically. 'It can't be nice to be just the also-ran. Or even back of the field of runners. No wonder he looks so grim.'

'Yes, it is unfortunate,' Rosselli agreed. 'Morgan never hides his feelings. He is not a diplomat.'

'Unlike you,' I thought, looking at his bland face and beautifully-tailored suit. A close friendship between him and the scowling, histrionic Grant seemed unlikely. No doubt their relationship was more in the nature of the author-agent dependence.

'And so,' concluded Rosselli, 'Miranda is sometimes pleased, because she feels important and she likes to feel that she has power over him. Other times he bores her. Sometimes she likes him. Probably she will go back to England and see many other men, and when she is bored with all of them she will marry this Robert Thornton who is so suitable.' His dismissive tone implied it was a predictable end to a rather trite affair, and I couldn't help agreeing.

'And now,' Stefano Rosselli went on, with an adroit change of subject—the Travers love-triangle was obviously of limited interest, and certainly not in the Romeo and Juliet class—'tell me what other parts of Italy you are going to see.' He smiled charmingly.

'Well,' Barry began, 'we haven't much time left, so I thought we'd motor to Umbria—we'd like to visit Assisi—and spend a couple of days there. Then Venice, and back to Rome to deliver the car to the car-hire firm and catch our plane for London. Which will give me about two days before starting back at work again.'

'Then may I wish you a very pleasant trip. I hope it doesn't rain.' He glanced at his watch. 'I am so sorry, I have an appointment and I must go. Let us hope that we will meet again—perhaps the next time you visit Florence? And I hope, Mr Vaughan, that your next book is not too difficult to write.' A bow, an ultracharming smile, the bill paid at the cash-desk, and he was gone.

And so were we, the next morning. A week later we were back in London, where I retrieved an ecstatic Bella (our dog) from the kennels, opened the mail, and prepared to launch myself into yet another temp job.

TWO

Dee

I WAS BACK IN Woodfield and back at work when the topic of Miranda Travers cropped up again. My erstwhile career as a magazine journalist folded up when the mag folded up, and I've been working off and on (more off than on) as a temp secretary ever since. Which has the advantage of variety, at any rate, my assignments varying from an oil company, to a PR firm, to a photographer. At the moment I'm in the property business. To be more precise, I work as general assistant three days a week to a letting agency, and it's surprising how busy we are. Their other branch in Highgate is coining it in, with no bedsit under £55 per week minimum rent, and whole houses being let out at phenomenal charges. Woodfield isn't in that bracket, but the rents are creeping up, not to mention the demand. After all, if you're in an area commutable to the big metropolis, with all mod cons—bus services a-plenty, supermarkets, restaurants and multiple shops, and green fields within driving distance—you've got it

made, if you want to let out your bijou attic room
for an exorbitant price.

Anyway, I wasn't actually *at* work when I saw
her picture in the mag. I was at the hairdresser's.
Sergio's, which is small and cosy and warm and
untidy, isn't cheap, but it's a hell of a lot cheaper
than The In-Place, over the road, one of these
streamlined chromium set n'blow dry factories, too
sleek to be chic, but too upmarket to be downprice.
Sergio occasionally wields the scissors himself, but
usually it's a feminine enclave, and Wendy, who
usually 'does' me, was occupied with a tinting job
and with recounting how she got her Wella di-
ploma. So I waited, sipping my polystyrene coffee,
and leafing through the mags from *Woman's Own*
to glossies. And there she was! Not alone in all her
glory, but one of a group photographed at one of
these social gatherings where bishops say things to
actresses and Lord Hefty-tum's eldest son swivels
hips opposite a punk.

She was smiling vaguely and wearing something
flowing and dark and medieval, and had her hair in
a snood. Guinevere alighted from her palfrey,
rather than Venus alighted from her shell, this time.
The gossip columnist referred to her (not unpre-
dictably) as 'beautiful top model Miranda Travers'
and made allusions to her current beaux—Thornton, top of the list, pursued by one Guido di Montefalcone and a couple of other bods. Morgan Grant

was not mentioned; not even as an also-ran. I wondered if Guido di Montefalcone was a racing driver or a rising Hollywood 'type'. Or more likely one of her Florentine acquisitions. The few lines on Miranda concluded with the information that she was 'spending Christmas in Sussex'. Probably, I thought, the Thorntons had a country mansion or an extended and converted oasthouse, or something, in that county—from which Miranda either might or might not emerge with an engagement ring on her finger. One reads between the lines. And at that moment Wendy advanced, scissors and Wella story at the ready, so I put the article away and prepared for a chit-chat.

'HAIL, DEARLY BELOVED,' Barry greeted me that evening, as I returned to the connubial central heating in Elmtree Avenue. I was somewhat pink of nose and laden with parcels, this being late-night shopping evening at the supermarket, and drear December to boot.

'Hail,' I returned, dumped the shopping in the hallway and sniffed hopefully. Barry, when home earlier than I, does the dinner, when he remembers—unless he's been grappling with his muse. 'Oh, good, you've done it.' Judging from the savoury aroma, muse remained ungrappled-with, and dinner was nearly ready for dishing-up.

'Woof.' Bella, our Schnauzer, added her greeting, and frisked around my ankles.

'Woof to you, too, sweetie.'

The purchase of Bella was my idea, but by this time Barry's just about as fond of her as I am. 'She is,' he pronounced recently, 'a dog of exceptionally sweet nature and exceptional intelligence.' Personally I don't think Bella, though undoubtedly a sharp little number, is quite in the canine superbrain class, but if Barry wants to think so, well, let him.

'You're looking revoltingly cheerful, Barry,' I commented, as my ever-loving uncorked a bottle of New Zealand Chardonnay and poured some into my waiting glass with a truly sommelier-like flourish. 'Even smug.'

'Ah.'

'A non-committal answer if ever I heard one. What gives? A rising A J P Taylor among the history students?'

'No.'

'You've finished writing *Framed Death?*'

'Nearly, but that's not it. Try again.'

I paused for the ritual racking of the brain, then shook my head. 'I give up.'

'I knew you would.'

And I knew he'd say that. Marital predictability!

'Well, go on, then, tell me.'

He paused to sharpen anticipation and suspense, and I obligingly leaned forward, agog.

'The first series is on offer to American TV.'

Proof of the Pudding etc, Barry's whodunnits, have previously been televised and received gratifyingly by the great British viewing public.

'Congrats, darling. Er—is American TV going to take it?'

'It's a pretty sure-fire thing. Not quite at contract stage, but nearly.'

'No wonder you look like the cat that got the cream.'

Barry loves writing his whodunnits, which are clever but make relaxing reading. They bring out a completely different persona in him, more jokey and less, well, ponderous than his Woodfield Tech lecturer's persona. We both loved the excitement and showbizzery which the televising of them brought, and, naturally, we are not unappreciative of the lovely lolly, which has made our mortgage a mere bauble rather than an Atlas-like weight, and has provided luxuries like holidays, half-term long weekends and bottles of plonk.

'So, in view of the pennies from Heaven which are due to descend in the near future, why not get another thingie, Dee?'

'Great! Ummm—an expensive thingie or a non-expensive thingie?' It's as well to know these things before one embarks on a search.

'An expensive thingie—within reason, of course,' he added hastily, just in case I was thinking along the lines of Leonardo cartoons or Fabergé eggs.

'Good.' I uttered a blissful sigh, and fed a generous dollop of succulent meat to Bella, who snuffled with equal bliss. It was bliss all round in the Vaughan household.

Barry and I don't always see eye to eye on expenditure, especially in the matter of feminine apparel, but fortunately he approves of what he calls 'Dee's thingies', which are items coming under the heading 'Antiques, and *Objets d'art*—in a small way. For example, the little Bilston enamel boxes, the Meissen figurine and my collection of single and paired plates—Dresden, Royal Worcester, Coalport. One day I'll get a Welsh dresser to put them on. More costly, the Regency card-table, the Drocourt corniche-cased carriage clock, the Georgian silver-and-gilt vinaigrettes and the Jacobean oak chest. The last-named reposes in glory on the top landing, where it houses sundry articles of linen, transferred from the quilted wicker basket, now donated to Help the Aged. I liked the quilted wicker linen-basket—but I like my dark panelled chest much better.

Barry and I are 'going up in the world', no doubt about it, and obviously the acquisition of things like this is one result. I can see, though, that it might become obsessive, so I keep an eye on myself. The carriage clock and the vinaigrettes were inherited, the card-table a gift from Barry, and the porcelain and the chest were paid for by quite a lot of hard labour at the agency and elsewhere. There are lots of other things I'd like, and I expect we'll acquire some of them over the years, but I can't really understand the mentality of people who'll do anything—even murder—for a Tanagra statuette or an original Impressionist painting. Or perhaps I do understand it.

'And what,' Barry suggested, over the coffee and biscuits, 'about Christmas away, this year? I mean, a whole week or so, if your employers will let you go for that time. No rushing round the shops at the last minute,' he pressed on. 'No Christmas dinner to prepare; just being waited on hand and foot. Away from the carbon monoxide fumes and the annual drunken orgies at number thirty-five, and the ever-present fear that some relative may descend on us. Christmas at leisure, in luxury, in the country, with congenial companions in an atmosphere of relaxed *joie de vivre*.'

'You should have been in advertising,' I remarked crushingly.

'That's what a lot of people say.' Barry remained uncrushed. 'Seriously though, Dee, doesn't it sound good?'

'Well, it sounds tolerable,' I admitted. 'Though I'm a bit suspicious about the congenial companions and the relaxed *joie de vivre*. May I ask, is this country establishment an abstract idea, or an actual place?' Barry has a habit of sometimes presenting one with a *fait accompli*. I think he caught it from me. Probably in self-defence.

'An actual place.'

'I thought so.' I poured out more coffee, put some water in Bella's drinking bowl, and waited for further information.

'It's in Sussex. East Sussex. Called The Grove—not very original, but there used to be a grove of larches or ash trees or something nearby. A private hotel with a difference, run by some acquaintances of Trevor's, a nice husband and wife. Well, he says they're nice.'

Trevor is Trevor Jones, the producer of the TV series of Barry's whodunnits. Which in fact had the overall title of 'Whodunnit?' He's Welsh, with dark curly hair and a slight paunch, and is given to enthusiasms. One of them is Barry. Obviously The Grove was another.

'What's the difference?' I enquired.

'Eh?'

'You said it's a private hotel with a difference.'

'Oh. Well, just that they only take people they know personally, or who are friends of friends and recommended.'

'Snob value. And they can't have a very large clientele—or else they've the most enormous circle of acquaintances.'

'Oh, that's only for Christmas,' Barry explained. 'You see, they don't have a large number of rooms, and they like to keep it a bit houseparty-ish. The rest of the year they operate normally. Of course,' he added, 'if you'd rather spend Christmas at home, that's all right by me. I just thought you'd like a change, and a rest.'

I dropped a kiss on the top of his head, as I started to clear the plates and cups away.

'That's very thoughtful of you, darling, and don't think I don't appreciate it. I suppose I feel Christmas is a family time, that's all, and I'd have to clear it with Mrs D.' (Mary Douglas runs the agency). 'But I would like a rest, you're right, and I like the houseparty-ish idea. There's one fatal flaw, though. What about Bella? I don't want to sound doting, but we did have to put her in kennels when we were in Italy, and we will for our next summer break, and I don't want the poor little creature to get unsettled and feel unloved and unwanted and so on.'

'No problem,' Barry announced cheerfully. 'Apparently there are facilities for dogs as well at The Grove.'

'Oh well...in that case...' Perhaps it really was a hotel 'with a difference'. 'I'll think about it.'

'Fine. What's on the box tonight, by the way?' And the conversation drifted into another channel.

It was later, in bed, where we had been driven

by a particularly stultifying documentary, that I remembered the article I'd been reading at the hairdresser's. I shoved my bookmark into my M M Kaye and dug Barry in the ribs with my elbow. He emerged from a somnolent inspection of the ceiling with a pained 'Ouch!'

'Guess who's going to be in Sussex this Christmas as well?'

'Oh, so you have decided to go, then?'

'I suppose so.'

'No, I can't guess. Andy and Fergie?'

'Not *quite* as newsworthy. *La Primavera* herself. Miranda Travers. *You* know—the girl we saw in the Uffizi,' I added, since Barry was looking slightly bemused.

'Oh, her.' His expression brightened reminiscently.

'Yes, her. I saw it in a mag at Sergio's—one of those party pieces on who's doing the Hokey Cokey with whom. Her name is still being linked, in inverted commas, with Robert Thornton. A guy called Guido di Montefalcone was mentioned also, and a couple of other swains-in-waiting, but Robbie-boy still seems to be top of the list.'

'Was the dour and drama-laden Morgan Grant mentioned?'

'Didn't rate even a half-line.'

'Bet he's simmering away somewhere in the background, though. I don't suppose,' Barry pointed out, with inescapable logic, 'that we'll bump into her. Or vice versa. Sussex is a big county.'

'True. So are most of the counties in England. But it's a bit of a coincidence, don't you think, Barry? I mean, first Florence, then Sussex.'

Barry grunted noncommittally. He obviously didn't think it was. Or wasn't interested. Maybe he was thinking out his end-of-term closing lecture on the issues involved in the American War of Independence. Or the career of Bismarck. Or even the Rinascimento, which he's been into enthusiastically since our Italian trip (I had to restrain him from trying to effect an introduction to Sir Harold Acton when we were in Florence). Or maybe he just wanted to go to sleep. I took the hint and abandoned conversation and M M Kaye, switching off the reading lamp with a sigh.

BY THE next evening Barry had contacted Trevor and found out the dog situation at The Grove; then he had contacted The Grove and spoken to mine host and hostess, Robin and Betty Brewer by name. Betty had a slight Devonian burr and confirmed that Bella would be more than welcome, and would find canine company in their own dogs, a Pyrenean sheepdog named Ajax, and a French poodle, Fifi. So Barry made a provisional booking, and it was confirmed after I'd cleared it with Mrs D, who said that I was quite welcome to extend my allotted four-day Christmas break to a week, or even ten days, as long as I made it up by working on Fridays for the next few weeks. Fair being fair, I agreed, so we were all set for one of those Christmasses that have become increasingly popular of late. Namely, you opt out of the carol singing, the local bazaar, stuffing the turkey, baking mince pies, and all contact with nearest and dearest, and make for a hotel pre-decked with holly and mistletoe and tinsel, where various other people in similar flight foregather. Colour televisions are laid on so that the Queen's speech and Disneytime and the other traditional compulsaries won't be missed, and organised festivities ensure that a jolly good time is had by all. Or, conversely, is not had at all. Don't knock it till you've tried it. I would, I decided, reserve judgement, and take along a notebook so I could start planning out and writing an article on our Italian jaunt—something along the lines of 'Travels without a Donkey' or 'Tuscan Trip' or even 'From Spaghetti Junction to Spaghetti land'. One should improve the shining hour. Also, it would prove a good excuse to retire from the fray from time to time should the junketing or the company not be to our taste.

'Bella, baby,' I told her, 'you're going on holiday.' Bella looked at me with her head on one side, bright eyes snapping, and wagged her tail.

'Woof, *woof,*' she commented enthusiastically.

'Well, I just hope you're not disappointed,' I said darkly. 'And that you'll get on with Ajax and Fifi.'

Bella shot me a pitying glance. She's right. I should curb these Cassandra-like pessimistic traits. She'll probably have a whale of a time and we'll be stuck with sending Christmas cards to Ajax and Fifi for the rest of our lives!

THREE

Dramatis Personae

Morgan

MORGAN GRANT stood, arms akimbo, in the centre of his studio, and surveyed the canvases in front of him. He swore, quietly but savagely, and repeatedly. After which he felt better. Not greatly better, but a bit better. He strode out of the studio, down three flights of narrow stairs, grabbed a duffel coat from a branched wooden coatstand and a string bag from a hook in the wall, and flung out of the front door in search of provisions.

Morgan's studio flat literally was that—a studio, perched in the roof, and a small bedroom, small sitting room, and shower room with toilet, below the studio. Kitchen and bathroom were shared with the other occupants of the house—Chris, a dispatch rider given to roaring off on assignments at night on his Honda, and Walter, a fifty-ish teacher, who owned the ground floor and middle floor, and sublet. He had owned the whole house, till he sold the top part to Morgan, who had been having a certain success at the time and had also been teaching in an art school in Central London. The move from Whitechapel to Highgate had been a shrewd one, though he still had twenty grand in mortgage to pay off. The house was in one of those sloping streets straggling downhill sideways from Highgate Village. Still pretty enough to be picturesque, with tangled back gardens and birdsong. Within a short walk there was a garden centre, full of rose bushes and shrubs and stone statuary. And it wasn't easy to find studios with skylights, particularly in areas which Dee Vaughan's Mrs D would have described (and did, in her ads) in purple prose.

Several times a day Morgan was drawn back to a fascinated contemplation of those same canvases, even if he were working on something else. They stood in a group of three, one full centre, the other two semi-circularly flanking it. The one in the centre showed Miranda Travers, in a sylvan setting, and in a flowing Botticellian gown similar to the one the Vaughans had seen her wearing in the Uffizi, with a chaplet of Spring flowers on her head and her hair flowing loose. The one on the left showed her as Dee had seen her in the magazine picture, in black velvet, medieval, with silver snood, à la Guinevere. And the one on the right was obviously pre-Raphaelite derivative, with Miranda as Ophelia, floating down a flower-strewn stream, fair tresses fanned out, and wearing a white and rather diaphanous shift. It managed to be both virginal and erotic, which no doubt was what the painter had intended.

In his most lucid-thinking moments, Morgan Grant would have been the first to admit that his attitude to Miranda Travers was mixed-up. On the one hand, she was not just a woman, but a recurring inspiration. Which meant that he regarded her in a high-handedly possessive light, not only as his occasional model, but as something that belonged to him. After all, an artist's inspiration does belong to him, doesn't it? On the other hand, Miranda remained perpetually, teasingly, beyond his reach. An independent and successful modern girl, educated as well as decorative, able to command large sums of money, and with a retinue of admirers she clearly intended keeping on a string and playing off against each other.

And now the perverse little vixen was off to the wilds of Sussex for Christmas—to 'get away from it all'. At least, on her rare and brief visits to the studio she would confide in him to some extent, even if this meant that she clearly regarded him as no longer anywhere near the running as a suitor, and meant to award him the consolation prize of friend. Thornton *fils*, under pressure from Thornton *père*, who wanted to see his son settled in a suitable country-house setting, with a couple of children and a dog and ponies, was pressing for an engagement,

and was understandably irritated by her cool statement that she didn't want to settle down *just* yet
'though you know, Robert darling, you're *the* most
important man in my life.'

On top of this, a new figure had entered the lists,
the result of a whirlwind romance during Miranda's
last days in Florence: Guido di Montefalcone, minor Italian nobility (his ancestors had been rather
disreputable and robber baron-ish back in the Cin-
quecento and still retained a castle in Umbria). Miranda had met and liked old Umberto, the father,
who in his way was just as formidable as Richard
Thornton, industrialist. Guido had a good income,
from varied and undefined sources, and since he
was the eldest son he'd succeed to the title of
Conte. He had two younger brothers, Cesare and
Francesco, who adored him and treated Miranda as
a kind of visiting goddess; and he was Latin and
passionate, given to extravagant gestures and extravagant changes of mood. At the moment his
quicksilver temperament appeared in favourable
contrast to the measured calm of Robert Thornton.
And he was courting Miranda, with, apparently, as
much firmness of purpose as Robert.

Back in the studio, Morgan threw a dust-sheet
over his three studies of Miranda and turned his
attention to the abstract he was currently working
on, pausing now and then to take a bite out of an
apple. A steak and kidney pie was heating up in

the kitchen oven and as he waited for it, a plan was forming in his mind. Rye was a picturesque town and he remembered staying in a boarding house there for a couple of days a few years ago. Somewhere he had the address and the phone number. They certainly wouldn't be overbooked this time of year and it was near enough to East Peasmarsh, where Miranda was going for Christmas, for him to make contact. Not that she would be pleased— the reverse. But, reasoned Morgan, chomping his apple, for once he would have stolen a march on Thornton and the others. As for what purpose it might serve—well, he knew Miranda well enough to realise that she had no intention of being pressurized into an engagement. If he could persuade her into giving Thornton the thumbs-down, that was the most serious contender removed from the scene. A Miranda unwed was infinitely preferable to a totally inaccessible Miranda. Besides which, Morgan reasoned virtuously, she would be hellishly unhappy with Thornton and he with her, once the novelty wore off. All in all, a few days in Sussex seemed a good idea.

Joyce

JOYCE BRADLEY walked along the corridor from Charing Cross Underground station. On each side of her posters flashed by advertising films, ballet, concerts, an art exhibition. Courses for this and courses for that. More films. She could hear the surge of thumping feet advancing resolutely, down the sloping walk she trod, up the sloping walk towards her. Young, old, middleaged. Multi-racial, multi-garbed. The lighting was bright and a boy with a long, black, flapping coat, open over dungarees and a stripey sweater, was playing the guitar—gentle, rippling music. Joyce was a softie for the buskers. Away from London for any length of time and she would feel a tugging at the heart, a lump in the throat, a stinging behind the eyes when she heard them again. There was so much to dislike about London, particularly these impersonal overcrowded days, but the buskers she loved, and they were one of her romantic associations with the city—grey, grimy London, with its splashes of colour, bright as a costermonger's oranges. And a raucous costermonger's shout to go with it.

Joyce paused, fumbled in her bag and slipped a fifty pence piece onto the bit of cloth spread waiting on the ground. There were a few other coins there. The boy looked at her vaguely. There was a twitch of the lips that might have been a brief acknowledging smile. Then, as she walked on down the tunnel, he concluded, stopped, and started a new tune, 'Killing Me Softly with Her Song', plangent and insistent. It lingered in her mind as she reached the British Rail station, even though she could no longer hear it.

On the train a vicar, floridly handsome, with a floppy bow tie, was discussing the problems of his parish with a woman in a Wetherall mac and matching cap. She looked—and sounded—the archetypal middle-class Englishwoman. Out of the window, Joyce saw a church steeple pierce a chilly grey sky, a weathercock perched firmly on its top. The train passed through a station called Hither Green, and a ticket collector with a charming smile said, 'good morning' in a burr, and punched their tickets. He was rubicund, fair-haired; the conventional picture of a countryman.

Opening her eyes after a snooze, Joyce caught the unexpected beauty of four swans sailing across a stretch of water, and then the train was at Paddock Wood. After that the neat, boxed semis gave way to red-brick and gabled houses, a spinney and farmhouses in the centre of pale brown fields soaked with puddles.

It was bleak December now, but she recalled her last trip down, in the gentle early autumn; the trees all warm golden shades and the sky blue, as the oasthouses of Kent gave way to those of Sussex. There had been ponies grazing; one of them a chestnut with four white socks. Beautiful. She sighed. She often wished she wasn't so susceptible to beauty—a chestnut pony, trees in autumn, a busker's music, snatches of Shakespeare. And Gabriel. Spending a weekend in Sussex with a friend, she had determined to come there again, and then she had been introduced to the Brewers, who ran a hotel that was a converted Georgian house, and who limited their Christmas guests to people they knew, or were acquainted with. So she'd booked herself and Gabriel in for the holiday. Neither of them had other plans. Gabe avoided his family and her own were scattered this long since. And they didn't want to stay in the flat—too cramping, too mundane, too everyday. She was checking into the hotel this evening and Gabriel was coming down tomorrow to join her.

Taking out her compact, Joyce applied a touch of lipstick and sighed again. She saw in mirrors an anxious, fading, rather plain middle-aged woman, dark hair scattered with dashes of grey. She missed the good bone structure, mobile lips and warm brown eyes that other people noticed more than occasionally. In her own estimation she looked just like a harassed school-teacher (which she was) and less than interesting.

If it had not been for a streak of stubbornness she would never have taken up with Gabriel Field. The same streak that had caused her to choose English and Music as her subjects, rather than Maths (so useful, you'll never lack a job, Joyce). And buy a flat she couldn't afford and which needed so much doing to it, but which was in a lovely old house in Kilburn and convenient to train routes for concerts and the theatre. Which is where Gabriel came in. He had started out her lodger (which he remained) but then became—what? Her toy boy? Sensitive, she imagined that must be what it seemed like to everyone and, to be realistic, that's exactly what it did seem like to many.

He was handsome as an angel, and young, and lived on a grant. He was studying for an MA and writing a thesis on something connected with the development of drama, which meant he 'kept in touch' and their lives were enlivened by various theatrical types popping in and out of the flat at odd moments. She was much older and owned the flat where she let him live for a reduced rent. Her job was unglamorous but reasonably well paid, and she frequently paid the tab on their outings. Besides, today, in the crude 1980s, many young men fell into the gigolo role without thinking much about it—especially those who had the kind of looks that Gabriel Field possessed, and not much else.

What most people didn't realise was that they were not lovers, in the generally understood sense. They didn't sleep together, though one might give the other a brief affectionate kiss sometimes, or pass an arm round the shoulders. She admired his looks and, more, his vibrant youthfulness, which made her feel young herself, and admired an independent, casual quality in him that didn't care what people thought of him and which kept him separate, un-owned by anybody. He tolerated her and was, she thought, fond of her; had been known to spring to her defence on a couple of occasions, pouncing angrily. But she didn't *really* know what he thought of her. Perhaps he even laughed at her sometimes, with a crony or two, especially if he'd downed a few whiskies. 'Good old Joyce'—she could imagine the tone of voice, patronising even if affectionate. But she didn't care—much. What she was afraid of was losing him. So she didn't think about it. The busker's music came back to her, hauntingly. 'Killing me Softly with her Song, Killing me Softly...' Was Gabriel killing *her* softly, without meaning to? Because if he went she was sure she'd fall into little cobwebby pieces, like brittle butterflies' wings.

But now the train was pulling into Rye Station and she was gathering together her suitcase and handbag, giving in her ticket, looking round for a taxi—yes, there was one, and no one else was making for it yet. Her spirits rose as she imagined a nice hot bath and then dinner.

Hal

MAJOR HENRY GARDNER, known as Hal to his intimates, of whom there were not many left, finished unpacking his suitcase and contemplated going down to the bar for a whisky and soda. He decided against it, and rang for one.

It was brought by Katy, a distant relative of the Brewers—a sturdy girl, moderately pretty, who performed her duties with a friendly smile but a slightly abstracted air, as if her mind was partly occupied with calculus or German syntax or chemistry formulae, or something equally abstruse. Hal supposed she was the maid, for want of a better word. Tonight she would be the waitress, probably assisted by another young woman. She wore a neat grey dress with a roll neck, and flat shoes in soft, comfortable-looking leather. The days of maids— or waitresses—in black, with white collar and cuffs and starched cap, seemed now to belong only in the realms of Galsworthy plays and outdated drawing-room comedies. Though he briefly recalled a Lyons Corner House in London which had revived the fashion. The Fannys and Hettys of a less advanced era had given place to the Mabels and Gladyses and Florries and Roses of more than yesteryear. 'Upstairs, Downstairs' on the TV—and *that* was going back a bit. Today the daily or weekend helps in suburban areas were most likely unemployed actresses and nurses, and the girls in places like The Grove were most likely studying for 'A' levels on the side. Today's Katies and Jeans would become tomorrow's Natashas and Fionas. And so it went on.

Major Gardner sat in the wing-chair by the window and sipped his drink in the gathering dusk. Warmth from the central heating flowed through him—now he was getting on he felt the cold more than ever. The furniture was good, solid, not shiny and new and gimcrack. There was even a little davenport in the corner. On the other hand the walls and ceiling were white-painted, fresh, the William Morris patterned curtains were new, there was an automatic teamaker with china on a tray, ready for the morning, complete with a choice of teabags and a carton of milk, and a radio with digital alarm on one side of the bed, pairing with the bedside lamp on the other. The Grove was very comfortable, no doubt about it, and the food, which included trawler-fresh seafood—a Sussex speciality—was excellent. But it was pricey, certainly by his standards.

Below him a wooden gate creaked, and then banged, as a figure flitted out of it. That woman who'd arrived earlier, he supposed—she'd started tramping round immediately, in slacks and sheepskin jacket, though what she found of interest in the vegetable garden which his window overlooked, he couldn't fathom. Probably killing time. Like himself.

Time lay heavy on the Major's hands now. Army life in India, where he followed in the footsteps of his father before him, was followed by an administrative post in Nigeria, and early retirement. His wife, Mary, was the English rose type, whose English rose complexion grew progressively sallower and more weatherbeaten under the rigours of the climates she lived in. Their children, James and Victoria—both born when Mary was past her first youth—had been public-school educated, the Gardners living in spacious government-provided accommodation abroad. On their rare leaves at home they would stay with relatives and, like many others, when they returned they found property too expensive and their income inadequate by any standards. However, Hal, who had quite a few contacts, found a job in an import-export concern and, though he grumbled it was glorified clerking, he trundled along in it without being unhappy for quite a few years. This enabled them to purchase the retirement bungalow with nice garden near Hastings, and to help James through university and pay Vicky's fees at St Godric's.

Then Mary had become ill and had died just before his final retirement, which meant the bungalow, though small, was lonely. Victoria was abroad with her boss—with whom she was in love—helping him to set up a branch of his business in Spain. And James, married with two children and a working wife, was living in Cumberland. They invited him there for Christmas and at Easter, but the Major, knowing how busy and harassed his daughter-in-law was, and how small the house was, considering her widowed mother would have to come too, had declined Christmas for the past couple of years, and gone to The Grove instead.

It had the advantages of solid comfort and a certain novelty—one didn't know quite who would be staying there. Last year's Christmas intake had included an advertising executive and his attractive wife, a Lancashire widow of ample proportions who had flirted pleasantly with the Major (still, at a pinch, 'a fine figure of a man' in his sixties) and a television comedian and his family. Robin Brewer had had some highly-paid technical job in television before he and his wife had come into possession of this place, and many of their guests, certainly the Christmas ones, were drawn from a loose but far-reaching net of contacts, most of whom had some connection with the television scene. So far the Major had seen only one other guest—the woman in the sheepskin jacket—but he gathered there were to be a couple of others by the evening and more arrivals the next day.

He finished his whisky and soda and glanced at his watch as he drew the curtains. Time for a snooze and a shower before going down to dinner—and a predinner drink.

Terence and Tony

'AND HOW LONG are we going to take, now?' enquired Terence Fitzgerald in plaintive tones. His companion carefully skirted a wobbly cyclist caught in the headlights before stepping on the accelerator.

'Not long. Possess your soul in patience.'

'I'd rather possess my dinner, thanks. I could eat an ox. Well—half an ox,' he amended.

'It's your own fault, me fine boyo. If you hadn't spent so long in the pub impressing that Lolita type with the cleavage with your whimsical charm, we'd have hit the road a lot earlier.'

'And aren't I trained to appreciate things of rare beauty?' retorted Mr Fitzgerald, uncrushed.

'And knockers like that are rare—I know. Still, if we miss dinner we both know whose fault it is.'

'Guilty, m'lud. I plead guilty. But just step on the gas a bit more, will you, Tony?'

Anthony Avery sighed noisily but obliged. He and Fitzgerald got on well on a personal level, as well as being business partners, the mercurial Irishman's blarney being a foil to Tony's more restrained, sardonic personality. Terence had a controlling interest in a shop in Dublin's Francis Street, which sold mainly Victoriana, but he was more taken up with his newest venture, The Treasure Trove in Brighton's Lanes, which had been surviving for the past two years and showing a healthy profit for the last one. It stocked what seemed to be a little of everything in the bric-à-brac line, from cameos and art deco to some genuinely rare and beautiful collectors' items, and was usually packed with browsers, most of whom ended up buying something, often more costly than they had intended. Avery owned a 40% share of The Treasure Trove, and Fitzgerald owned a 40% share of Avery Antiques in Rye, a far more sedate concern. So, in theory, the losses of one were bolstered by the gains of the other, either way, which was fine as long as they weren't both running at a loss at the same time. On the whole it seemed to be working so far. Of the two, Anthony was the connoisseur, the specialist; Terence the inspired magpie.

They had both decided to stay near to their respective shops over Christmas, ready for an early return to business, and had ended up booking at The Grove. Terence was unmarried, thirty, with a flock of casual girlfriends and a vast clan of relatives in Dublin and elsewhere. Anthony was in his late thirties and also unmarried.

Having 'stepped on the gas', they arrived at the

hotel in time to wash and brush up and share a pre-dinner drink at the bar with a military type who seemed to greet their appearance with some relief.

The first Christmas guests had arrived.

FOUR

Barry

DEE AND I were all set to enjoy our Christmas break. So was Bella. Life isn't, after all, very exciting for a dog at Elmtree Avenue. Safe, perhaps, but not what you'd call stimulating. Which I suppose is why she seemed to enjoy the kennels we left her in when we went to Italy. A change from the daily routine, which involves being on her own quite a bit three days a week when Dee is at Flatfinders. Not that it's easy to get a dog into a kennels. Even a little dog, like Bella. If you don't believe me, just try it. It's like trying to get membership of an exclusive club. Or getting into the January sales. You just join the queue. Mind you, once they know you, and always assuming your dog hasn't blotted its copybook during its sojourn, it's easier the second time round.

With Bella on the back seat of the car, however, making gratified little woof-y noises and gazing out of the window with great interest at the disappearing scenery, I was glad we'd brought her along. Dee was looking forward to some country walks, weather permitting, both for Bella's sake and her own—she announces the appearance of an extra unwanted inch round her waist, and spreading in other areas. Personally, all Dee's areas are all right by me just as they are, but women do seem to have this thing about weight. A few cuddlesome curves and they're convinced they're all set for the Fatty of the World stakes. Dee says darkly that a cuddlesome curve one day means the dreaded cellulite the next, and that when one is a trim five foot three one has to work at staying trim, or else. Maybe she's right.

Anyway, before we set off we had a day up in London, watching a performance of *The Importance Of Being Earnest* at the Edmund Kean School of Drama. In case this seems an odd pre-Christmas activity I should explain that Dee's niece Sally is a student at the Edmund Kean (which isn't *quite* in the RADA class, but definitely has cachet) and Sally was playing the part of Gwendolen. Which she did beautifully, all mannered, statuesque grace and cuttingly languid drawl. In real life Sally is unremittingly good-natured and positively overflowing with the milk of human kindness. Odd how a lot of women who yearn to play bitches are.

Sally got into the Edmund Kean (which is like the kennels in that it also has a waiting list) through the good offices of Dee's friend Zoe Zabrowski, who's a pillar of Woodfield thespian activity. She played Hedda in the past and I believe it's going to be Medea this year. Zoe wasn't there to enthuse over her protégée, however, because she was off in Kusadasi (or was it Dubrovnik?) where her husband Stan, a delicatessen tycoon, had played Santa with a summer home for Christmas. Summer homes are very 'in' at the moment, and I suppose when you consider that a house on one of the obscurer Greek islands or a modest villa in Turkey comes cheaper than a one-third share in a downmarket slum flatlet in London, you can see why. Anyway, having duly congratulated Sally and joined her and her parents for the wining and dining session afterwards, we had completed all our obligations and were ready to hit the road.

EAST PEASMARSH is a few miles out of Rye. There are a couple of pubs serving meals en route, and a minimarket which is really an extended village store. Otherwise there are miles of rolling Sussex Downs and sheep. Lovely houses are abundant— white clapboard and Snow White red brick, overgrown with shaggy creeper and sporting tall, tall chimneys with wisps of smoke curling out. And picturesque large detacheds with hedges and white stake fencing and drives. And a few new built-to-blend-in-harmoniously houses. And little rows of stone workmen's cottages, and picture-postcard oasthouses nestling in the middle of gently rounded slopes. The occasional tractor jolts its way over a ploughed field or up a lane.

The local bus service departs once every two hours, we found later, and the last bus back departs from Rye at 4.00 p.m., so it was just as well we had the car—a poor thing but mine own, and suitable for a history teacher, being on the aged side, though strong and full of fight. I could afford to replace it, but somehow I'd feel like Brutus raising the knife to Caesar. As long as it's going more or less satisfactorily, we'll keep it. After all, it took us on bed and breakfast tours round the West Country in less palmy, pre-Whodunnit days. Well done, good and faithful servant, and all that.

Anyway, we arrived *sans* hassle at The Grove, an imposing three-storeyed Georgian house with a sweeping driveway, and were welcomed by Robin Brewer and his wife Betty, who were as cheerful and welcoming as you'd want a hotelier and his missus to be. Obviously dog-lovers, they extended an even warmer welcome to Bella. Dee explained that we wanted Bella to sleep in our room, but that we'd like to leave her in their charge during mealtimes and when we went anywhere except walkies, and during any hotel activities where dogs would be *non persona grata.*

'That's all right,' Betty said reassuringly. 'You can give her to me in the morning and collect her any time you want. We have a ground-floor flat, so we've got some privacy, but we're on call when needed, even when you can't see us around the place. The number's written on the board above the reception desk, so you can phone through. And if there's any emergency at night—fire, or someone ill, or anything—we can be reached. The front door's locked at eleven, by the way, and all staff go off duty before then, but if anyone goes to a do and wants to get in later than that, there are some keys to the side entrance, so all you have to do is apply to Robin or me.' She smiled at us, a plump, fair-haired woman with a peaches and cream complexion that the passing of time (she must have been in her forties) had not wrecked.

'That sounds like a good arrangement, Mrs Brewer.'

'Oh, and I thought we were on first-name terms. I'll be very hurt if you don't call me Betty. Now I'm sure both of you would like to see your room— it's number ten upstairs, looking out over the lawn. And when you feel like it, perhaps you'd like coffee in the lounge, and I'll introduce you to a couple of the other guests.'

'Woof, woof,' interposed Bella sociably, and Dee laughed.

'She wants to make friends too.'

'So she shall then. I'll take her to meet our two and give her a snack. Robin, can you take the luggage up to number ten.'

'The luggage' comprised one small case (mine), one larger (Dee's—with different shoes and woollies and frillies; she always travels more laden than I do) and Dee's vanity case, which she carried herself. Packed with lotions, lipstick, a paperback Simon Brett and ditto Jonathan Gash, and a new blockbuster. Wreathed in tinsel and holly, watercolours by local artists hung on the wall by the stairs, and a small Christmas tree with coloured lights sat in a green tub at the top, to match the large tree in a red tub in the lobby below.

Number ten had a powder-blue carpet and peacock-blue curtains, a solid-looking double bed and dressing-table, a built-in wardrobe painted white and a gorgeous carved oak armoire. There was an armchair and a wooden rocking-chair with cushions, and an exquisite little veneered escritoire in the corner. Dee uttered a cry of delight when she saw it. The Brewers looked gratified.

'Well, with you being a writer... We loved your series, by the way. Trevor said he'd had more fun doing it than anything else he's ever done. Hard work, but a barrel of laughs, he said.'

'How thoughtful of you—the desk, I mean.' I sighed inwardly. The Fates seemed to be conspiring that I should complete *Framed Murder* rather than concentrate on stuffing myself with roast turkey and plum pud and having a jolly good knees-up and watching telly.

As if he read my thoughts, Robin said, 'This is one of the largest rooms, so you share a bathroom with number nine, and there isn't a TV in the room, I'm afraid, but there's the one in the lounge whenever you want to watch. Most people do tend to on Christmas Day and Boxing Day, though we try to get games and things going as well, and usually people enjoy them.'

Looking out of the window, onto a terraced walk, flowerbeds and an extensive lawn, with a small garden shed near the hedge separating lawn from road, I saw two people playing croquet. One wore slacks, a reefer jacket and a headscarf.

'Who's that?' asked Dee facetiously. 'The Queen?'

'No, she's at Sandringham.' Robin was deadpan, making me remember he'd had years of experience of media people, not to mention their jokes. Betty might be the jolly, warmhearted Devonian country lass, but it would be Robin who kept things running smoothly and saw to the publicity angle. 'Maybe another year. We take corgis too.' Dee grinned, and Robin added, 'That's Joyce Bradley. She's a teacher, a pleasant person but she worries too much. She seems to be enjoying the break from London.'

'Who's her companion?' Dee wanted to know.

'Gabriel Field. And he *is* her companion. They're a couple—sort of. Now I'll be getting

along. Betty will show you the bathroom, and
there's coffee and biscuits in the lounge, or tea and
toast and cake if you'd prefer it, any time you like.'
And he was off, before he could be tempted into
any further indiscretions about the two on the lawn.

The sun was shining and it was gloriously mild
for December. Gabriel Field was fair-headed and
wore a thick Arran polo-neck and blue jeans, with
calf-length leather boots. He looked up just at that
moment and saw us at the window, and gave a
cheery wave. Dee waved back, then we followed
Betty, who had settled Bella in her quarters, along
the corridor to the bathroom. This proved to be
enormous, patterned in white tiles with blue sea-
urchins and fishes on them, and flanked by an out-
size linen-cupboard stacked with soft woolly towels
on one side, and a shower-room on the other. Number thirteen was at the very end of the corridor, and
beyond it a twisting stairway led up to the top floor.

'It's store-rooms up there,' Betty explained.
'And a sort of office. There are two bedrooms, but
we don't use them much, because they haven't got
en suite bathrooms and the bathroom on the top
floor hasn't been modernized yet, so people aren't
so keen to be put there. Later we'll do more with
the top floor, but at the moment we're just a small
hotel—none of your weekend conference centre
and that.'

By the time we'd unpacked the cases and got

ourselves down to the lounge, with a bit of a nose-around en route, we'd got the hang of the geography. On the ground floor was the lounge, to the right of the reception desk—or to the left of the entrance, whichever way you looked at it. On the other side were a bar and the dining-room, which was partly panelled and had a large polished mahogany table in the centre, and smaller tables covered in red tablecloths grouped around. There were French windows with gold-tasselled red velvet curtains, and a lovely moulded ceiling. It looked out onto a gravelled walk, with stone urns, and grassy banks descending to lawn, and a small copse—hardly even that, just a knot of trees. The dining-room was separated from the drawing-room by panelled sliding doors. Beyond them, another high-ceilinged room, this one with a beautiful Adam mantel over an open fire with logs burning in it. Since there was also central heating we guessed this was special for Christmas. The carpet was pale green Chinese with a border of pale pink flowers, and cretonne-covered sofas and armchairs continued the green-and-pink motif. As in the dining-room, there was also wall-bracket lighting, each with cream and pale yellow shades, and a large ornate chandelier in brass hung in the centre—the only thing in the room which Dee considered out of place.

I thought it was rather hideous myself, though I

daresay it was worth a lot. Christmas cards scattered on the bureau-bookcase and on occasional tables provided bright splashes. More French windows looked out onto grassy banks, a flight of stone steps flanked by two stone urns—probably filled with anemones or something in the fine weather, but now lamentably empty—and the lawn. A wooden stepladder beside the upper window and some pieces of holly pinned onto moss-green velvet curtains showed that the Christmas decorations hadn't yet been completed.

Opposite the dining-room were kitchens, and beyond that a corridor leading to an end door, with rooms one, two, three and four beyond the drawing-room. Since the rooms on our corridor started at number eight, I guessed five, six and seven were in the flat which was obviously in the wing beyond the door.

In the lounge, we were introduced to the other occupants—the couple we'd seen already on the lawn, an elderly gentleman called Major Gardner, and two rather good-looking men, who apparently were both in the antiques business. When Dee found that one of them—the one called Tony—had a shop in Rye she brightened, and before long was deep in discussion of tallboys and Queen Anne and French provincial and what-not. I was collared by the Major, who turned out to be nearly local. That is, if you consider Hastings and its environs as nearly local. In fact, he proved a much more entertaining conversationalist than he looked, and we were soon deep in a discussion of local history.

'And,' concluded the Major, 'the fact that William set up an altar to Harold in Battle Abbey surely proves that he was stricken by conscience.'

'Oh, I don't know,' objected antique dealer number two, who was distinctively Irish in feature and slightly so in accent. 'After all, he didn't give the land back to the Saxons, did he? Any more than the Anglo-Normans gave their plunder back in Ireland—though my ancestors were among them, and they did all right out of it, I must admit. Anyway, praying for your defeated opponent seems to have been a stock thing—look at Henry IV and the chantry where they sang masses for Richard's soul.'

They wrangled cheerfully for a couple of minutes, while the woman from the lawn—now changed into a royal-blue woollen dress with one of those old-fashioned diamond half-moon brooches on it—drifted over, a bit timidly, to listen in.

'What do you think, Joyce?' demanded Terry, putting an arm round her shoulder and giving her a crinkly, twinkly smile. 'Say you're on my side, do!'

Joyce blushed slightly, and looked as if she didn't know whether to be gratified by the arm resting carelessly round her or to extricate herself.

'Well—I am, as a matter of fact, Terry. I think William set out to do what he intended when he invaded England, and he certainly didn't have the slightest qualm of conscience about it. An altar to Harold acknowledged a brave opponent and probably mollified the Saxons a bit. Standard lip-service.'

'I stand defeated.' The Major laughed. 'Do you know Rye, Barry? It's a fascinating little town.'

'Not very well.' I remembered it quite well, as it happened, but it kept the conversation flowing as the old gentleman waxed enthusiastic about the smuggling history of the Mermaid Inn and the fact that there was a copy of the register of the birth of Fletcher, the dramatist, in the parish church.

'There are various churches, of course; besides C of E there's a United Reform with Methodist in Church Square, and a nice Italianate R C nearby, too. Fletcher's father became Bishop of London, apparently. The Landgate's medieval, of course— like the original Mermaid, which was just clay and wattle.'

'It's a charming place,' Joyce agreed. 'Apparently various writers have thought so too—though I suppose Henry James is the most famous.'

'Mr. Vaughan seems to have joined the list,' came a voice from the other group, and I looked up to see the speculative, slightly sardonic gaze of the man called Tony fixed on me.

'I understand from our revered Betty that Barry here writes whodunnits, no less! Are you collecting material, Barry?'

Everyone looked at me with interest, and I felt annoyed at being singled out as 'visiting celebrity'.

'No,' I replied coolly. 'That is, I'm engaged on one, yes, but I've got my material already.'

'Well, that's a relief. I think I'd view being a character in a whodunnit with mixed feelings.'

'I wouldn't mind being a nice one,' volunteered Joyce, smiling at me.

'Ah, but who's to say he'd see you as nice, sweetie?'

'Of course he would.' Support came unexpectedly from the excessively handsome young man who had been lounging against the wall looking bored up to now. Obviously he had been following the conversation more keenly than one would have imagined. 'Wouldn't you?'

I wasn't sure if it was an appeal or a challenge. 'Of course. Joyce would probably appear as a very charming and intelligent minor character. If a crime was committed in a setting like this.'

'Which, of course, is unthinkable.'

I refused to let the sardonic Tony needle me into a denial and an exposé of the well-worn thesis that crimes can be committed anywhere, given motive, means and opportunity.

After a bit more desultory chat, Dee and I excused ourselves and collected Bella, looking smug and well-fed, from Betty. The sun had gone, and an evening chill was setting in, so we just went down the lane near The Grove, and back, Bella yapping away from time to time as she inspected some new sight or smell.

When we had delivered her back to our room and changed, it was time for a drink at the bar as we waited for seven o'clock dinner. This time Dee was nabbed by Major Gardner and I found myself hob-nobbing with Terry, who seemed a likeable, friendly type. Then our attention was distracted by a commotion at the front entrance. A taxi-man staggered in with a very large, white leather case and deposited it on the floor with a thump. He was followed by a vision in a white, ankle-length leather coat with a hood, trimmed with white fur, the ensemble completed by white boots and white gloves. The girl shook back the hood and a flow of long fair hair fell around her shoulders and down her back. She marched up to the desk and grabbed the register.

'I'm a bit late, but I had to wait for a taxi.' The voice managed to imply this was an unusual occurrence in its owner's life. 'It doesn't matter, though, does it? I mean, I did order dinner for eight.'

Dee spluttered into her Martini and I caught her eye.

'Do you see what I see?' she hissed, in a stage whisper. 'So who said Sussex is a big county?'

No prizes for guessing that the Snow Queen was *La Primavera*—little Miss Miranda Travers in person—at The Grove for Christmas.

FIVE

Miranda

MIRANDA TRAVERS enjoyed her entrance into the hotel. She usually enjoyed making an entrance, and it was very rarely that she was not conscious of creating a sensation. She also enjoyed the home-made carrot soup, mixed seafood and selection of vegetables and fruit salad, washed down with a good white wine and followed by coffee and the cheeseboard.

She was on this occasion dining alone, since everyone else had elected for the early dinner, but as she ate she was acutely aware of the presence of other guests in the lounge nearby. One of them, a good-looking fairhaired boy, came and poked his head round the dining-room door to ask her if she'd care to join them for a hand of cards later. She declined, but with her sweetest smile.

'I think I'll have a bath and an early night, but thanks all the same. I'll see you sometime tomorrow, I expect. My name's Miranda, by the way. Miranda Travers.' She looked questioningly at him.

'Gabriel Field. By the way, unless they haven't

told you yet, the bus only goes from here every two hours, so, if you want to go anywhere tomorrow, before it all closes down over Christmas, ten o'clock's the best time.'

'Thanks again.'

He nodded and disappeared, and she looked after him speculatively. True, she was off in 'the country' to 'get away from all that', but a harmless little flirtation with someone round her own age might be a refreshing change. There was no doubt about it, it was lovely to get away from cameras and photographic sessions and 'darling's' and tantrums (even her own), and the whole glamour scene which, once one was used to it, was either hard work or pseud. Even tacky. Not that she should knock it—it had given her maximum exposure, lots of parties, travel (granted, there were nicer things to do than stand in a harem suit under a palm tree in a desert, but lots of it *had* been exciting) and the admirers. Like Robert. And Guido. And how nice to escape from both of them, and to have herself a real merry little Christmas in the kind of place no one would ever associate with Miranda Travers.

She was beginning to realise that she had sold herself—to the media. And now she was contemplating selling herself again, in the good old, time-honoured fashion well known to Jane Austen and her contemporaries (even if Austen observed at one remove), and still current today, under all the 'career' and 'free love' and 'womens' lib' trappings.

Miranda remarked what happened to your average liberated career woman today. She got lumbered with a demanding job, a demanding *and* complacent husband and demanding kids, as well as running the home and frequently part-time courses and parents and in-laws who complained if they weren't visited and invited. In other words, the all-purpose skivvy, geared to computer-like efficiency without having replaceable electronic parts. And Miranda had passed from initial admiration to pity tinged with contempt. Since, she reasoned, she had been endowed with the grey matter to take her through the education system with reasonable results and the looks and social *savoir-faire* to make her both eminently desirable and 'suitable', why waste these assets on someone who would have her worn-out by the time she was thirty?

It was all a matter of common sense and of picking and choosing. But she was having a bit of a problem choosing, and she was suddenly beginning to panic about the loss of freedom and to wonder just how badly she would miss her contemporaries—either the college students she remembered nostalgically or the few people on the modelling scene she had liked and had crazy fun times with at discos and non-stuffy youth-appeal parties. Selling oneself into marriage with the 'right' kind of partner was a necessary evil, but the lesser of all evils, and she was prepared to work at making it work. Still... Miranda spooned fruit salad into her pretty mouth and wondered if Gabriel Field was fun. And if she'd have anything in common with him, other than youth and good looks.

Her room, she had noted wryly, was number thirteen. That plump woman who ran the place had apologised for the number and offered to put her into number twelve instead. But Miranda disliked being tagged as 'the type who'd make a fuss'—even though she frequently *did* make a fuss—so she had coolly refused the offer.

'It really doesn't matter. I'm not superstitious. It's not worth the bother of changing.' She wasn't particularly superstitious, as it happened, though one of her more endearing traits was her attachment to a small battered cloth panda called Wilberforce, which travelled with her as her mascot.

Number thirteen had its own bathroom and was one of the rooms with a TV, so Miranda was able to watch a variety show in bed, while sipping a hot toddy. There was a bar downstairs, but she found it more convenient and ladylike to travel round with a small supply of liquor. Bad for the complexion, perhaps, but good in the near-Arctic conditions she'd sometimes had to endure on the modelling circuit.

She particularly remembered one hotel in Scotland, situated beside a picturesque loch… And Yorkshire, where she had realised how apt a title *Wuthering Heights* was and decided the Bronte sisters must have been as tough as old boots (though none of *them* had had to do parachute jumps on the moors clad only in an acrylic cat suit).

The Grove was cosy and centrally heated to a nice fug, and her bath had been piping hot, but by this time Miranda was used to her nightcaps, cold or no cold, and there is no doubt that a generous drop of Haig (Miranda was never vague when she asked for it) helped to banish the spectre of her marriage. But it did not always banish dreams and that night she had a dream that turned into a kind of nightmare, where Santa Claus presented her with a parcel she couldn't unwrap and which was taken from her by a sinister man in a black mask.

A YAPPING NOISE along the corridor awoke her (Bella greeting the new day) and after tea in bed listening to a record-choice programme on the radio she was feeling OK, memories of nocturnal Santas and masked thugs forgotten.

It was a bright, sharp day, frosty but healthy, and she put on a pale blue angora dress and a white satin Alice band that made her look like one of the angels in a Nativity play. She tucked into sausages, kidneys, crisp bacon, tomato and fried eggs with the kind of appetite any angel would have considered unbecoming and excessive. Again, she was later than the other residents, unless they were still in bed, apart from an elderly gent sitting by the window. He gave her a courtly, old-fashioned bow, and she automatically flashed on the charming smile. Gabriel, she decided with annoyance, had probably gone into Rye—the nearest town of any note—but she was wrong. She collided with him in the corridor as she came out of the dining-room, and he brightened at the sight of her.

'Come and help us decorate for Christmas. In here.'

He caught hold of her hands and drew her into a large living-room, where another man, dark-haired and also handsome, was perched on top of a ladder doing something complicated with paper lanterns and tinsel. More decorations littered the floor.

Miranda sank gracefully into a chair, and jumped up again quickly with a loud 'Ouch!'

'What's the matter?'

'I sat on some holly,' she said, after investigating.

Gabriel laughed.

'It's not funny. It hurt,' she said indignantly.

'Well, better some prickles in your ass than in your temper. Hand it up to Terry, he'll pin it on the curtains out of harm's way. Here's a pot of paste and scissors and crepe paper. Can you help me make paper chains?'

'I suppose so.' He reminded her of the students she had been thinking about the day before. Some of them had just not noticed her looks after a bit, or hadn't been bothered anyway. They'd been matey, cavalier, *fun*. Robert would have been solicitous if she'd sat on holly; Guido might have been amused, but he'd have covered it with some flowery Italian remark. She found herself concentrating on the paper chains in companionable silence, while on the ladder Terry pinned up the offending holly and whistled 'On the first day of Christmas my true love sent to me...'

He broke off after a couple of minutes to enquire 'Where's Joyce?'

'Out with Dee and the dogs. Fifi's having a job to keep up. The trouble with getting anywhere near lawns and fields and lanes is that Joyce will start going in for this unremitting physical activity.'

'Who's Joyce?' Miranda demanded.

'My landlady, companion, mentor and friend. I'm extremely fond of her—but I like to get away to enjoy myself doing wicked or frivolous things sometimes. Especially on holiday.'

Miranda found herself nodding understandingly. She felt like that with Robert. Frivolous things were so carefully planned with him they lost their spontaneity.

'You're very pretty,' came the voice from the ladder. 'Quite beautiful, in fact. But then, I suppose a lot of people tell you that, so it's not the disclosure of the century.'

Miranda looked up, to meet the familiar, man-sees-girl-he-fancies regard. 'No, it isn't. I'm a model, anyway, so being attractive is my livelihood. It's—useful. But then, neither of you two are exactly ugly, so you must know for yourselves what it's like.'

Gabriel laughed. 'She's got you there, Terry, you old ladykiller.'

'She has that. Listen, Miranda, we three seem to be the young guard in this place. So I reckon it's up to us to organise things with Robin Brewer. Fun and games and Christmas spirit and so on. Pass-the-parcel and hunt-the-slipper and murder-in-the-dark and singing Christmas carols and whatever else you like to think of. Care to join us?'

Miranda found herself agreeing, and the next few hours were spent pleasurably, chatting, preparing paper games and ideas for charades and finishing the decorations. Joyce Bradley had joined them for a few minutes, but had been banished lightly and kindly by Gabriel, who told her to put her feet up, read her Agatha Christie, and leave them to get on with the work.

'Oh dear, now she's hurt,' sighed Terry, who had seen her face. 'Shall I call her back?'

'No, don't. Hard cheese,' said Gabriel. 'She'd only get in the way and feel out of it, and more hurt. She'll enjoy the games and things when we get going. Joyce likes parties if they're small and she knows the people. She's shy, that's all.'

'Well, I suppose you know best.' Terry was doubtful. 'Look, where shall I put this?' He held up a piece of mistletoe.

'What about the chandelier?' suggested Miranda. 'I mean, it kind of stands out. If you pin it with all that holly, no one will notice it.'

'Good thinking. Gabe, help me get this stepladder over to the centre and hold it for me, will you? It's a bit wobbly.'

The mistletoe was duly tied to the central stem of the chandelier with a piece of green ribbon. Finally, they'd finished. The long, elegant room looked cheerful and festive. The Brewers were called in to admire, which they did, clucking and protesting that they'd meant to finish the decorations themselves that afternoon.

'But this is really artistic, isn't it, Betty? Far better than we could have done.

Betty agreed enthusiastically, the trio looked smug, and coffee and sandwiches were consumed all round.

CROQUET ON the lawn with Terry, Gabriel and Barry, who had joined them after a spell of re-

reading his unfinished *Framed Murder* manuscript, sweetened Miranda's temper still further, and since Joyce and Dee, having returned from their walk with the dogs, had cast a glum look at the croquet group and decided to go to Rye for lunch, Miranda was reigning queen bee supreme by lunchtime, with the Major and Anthony Avery added to the ranks of attendant males. Add coffee, liqueurs and Bendicks chocolates in the drawing-room, with the log fire crackling away merrily in the Adam fireplace, as if to balance the soft drizzle which had started outside, and a game of Trivial Pursuit produced by Terry, and Miranda was beginning to feel that her random choice of venue for Christmas (a choice made purely on impulse after a conversation with a modelling friend who 'adored Sussex' and knew someone who knew someone who had stayed at The Grove and pronounced it 'restful') was not as half-baked as she had begun to fear.

One game of Trivial Pursuit led to others, and though Barry and Tony Avery got the top scores, Miranda acquitted herself reasonably well. But as time passed, and Gabe started to look at his watch and wonder aloud about Joyce's whereabouts, it occurred to her that it might be a good idea to break up the game while she was still queen bee supreme. So she swept off to her room with the excuse of writing letters, although in fact she just lay down and listened to her Sony Walkman.

One outside call was put through to Miranda Travers that afternoon. It was from Robert Thornton, who had, unsurprisingly, tracked her down, and who demanded, in the firm and forceful tones that Miranda, earlier in their relationship, had hailed as 'deliciously masterful', that she should at least spend Christmas Day *chez* Thornton.

Miranda billed and cooed and 'darling'ed—and refused, sweetly but firmly. If matters with Robert took their likely course, she would be faced with a lifetime of Christmas Days *chez* Thornton, and she was not at all sure that the prospect pleased. This Christmas Day, at least, she would remain free, solo and gloriously *sans* Thorntons in any shape or form.

It did not disturb her unduly that Robert put the receiver down with a bang at the other end when she was midway through a trilling laugh. Poor Robert always cut up rough when he did not get exactly what he wanted, when he wanted. It was a trait that was familiar to Miranda since she possessed it herself. Nevertheless, she was beginning to feel that a married future in which recurring headaches played a not inconsiderable part might be advisable. Of course, if Robert became too caveman and unbearable, there was always divorce. The Thornton empire had been built by shrewdness as well as forcefulness, but on the other hand Robert was sometimes surprisingly generous, and there were always clever lawyers ready to become the Marvin Mitchelson of London.

She wondered if Robert had bought her anything for Christmas. Yes, of course he had, but in view of her defection she might not get it, or not till after the festive season anyway. Just as she was about to put her headphones on again and turn to Capitol Radio, the phone rang again. This time it was an internal call, from Reception.

'Miss Travers, there's a...special delivery parcel for you. Could you possibly come down and sign for it, please?'

She could and she would. Miranda was a girl who regarded presents, preferably expensive ones, as her lawful tribute, but she was not yet blasé enough to look on each received as 'just one more', and her heart still gave a schoolgirl's leap of antic-ipation on occasions like this.

As Miranda approached the reception desk an odd sight greeted her. Standing in front of the desk was a rather small Santa Claus, red-suited, white-bearded, with black shiny boots, and drops of rain dripping from the ends of his sleeves and the ends of his moustache. As she paused and stared at him, he trotted over and held out a square parcel and a paper attached to a clipboard.

'Sign, please.'

Miranda dutifully signed, and the Santa returned the paper to a satchel on his back. At the same time he switched on a square black cassette-player hung round his front on a black cord, and a short miscellany of Christmas tunes echoed out.

Katy, behind the reception desk, exchanged an amused glance with Miranda, as 'Silent Night', courtesy of the choir of King's College, Cambridge, was succeeded by 'Jingle Bells', and the small Santa, obviously getting the message that all was not quite as intended, hastily pressed the forward button on the cassette-player. A crackle vied with the sound of a loo flushing as a door opened down the corridor, then the sound of Guido's voice, sonorous, sexy and full of feeling.

'Buon Natale, mia bellissima Miranda.' And then, in English, fetchingly accented, 'May the value of my gift remind you of your value to me, now and forever.'

Katy looked suitably impressed, though the occupants of the lounge were, regrettably, glued to the television set and missed this touching declaration.

The small Santa bowed and made for the front door. Out of the long window they could see him swing himself onto a red motorbike and as he made off down the gravelled drive the roar of the bike was clearly audible.

'Well!' breathed Katy. 'That's the first time we've had a Santagram!'

'More of a Santagift.' Miranda gazed speculatively at the parcel in her hands. It could be jewellery, of course, but it seemed remarkably heavy, somehow, for a bracelet, or even a necklace.

'What's in it, I wonder?' Katy looked hopefully at Miranda, willing her to open the present on the spot. This, in spite of the comic note produced by 'Jingle Bells' et al, was romance on a Mills and Boon scale.

'Haven't the faintest. I'll open it later…sometime.' And Miranda, feeling she had established just the right note of careless nonchalance, spun neatly on her heel and drifted, ethereally, up the stairs. Katy stared after her with a compound of admiration, envy, thwarted curiosity and annoyance.

'Bitch,' she murmured. 'Cool, though.'

In her room, Miranda surveyed her gift. Wrapping paper and cardboard lay strewn around the floor. At first she had been disappointed, but looking at it, poised in beautiful simplicity on the dressing-table, she was impressed. It was beautiful and even if a reproduction, obviously valuable. Her art education had not been wasted, nor all those hours drifting through Italian galleries and museums. Briefly, she wished Morgan were here to show it to. Perhaps she'd give him a call and tell him about it.

When she'd ripped open the manilla envelope containing Guido's note and the provenance of her gift, she was even more excited. In the scales of eligibility, Robert Thornton—industrialist, clubman and prospective lord of the manor—wavered and slowly moved down a few inches; while Guido di Montefalcone—nobility, charming, fun to be with, rich enough, and with little baubles like this strewn round the ancestral home—ascended till the two figures balanced each other equally. Miranda sighed. She supposed she should put her beautiful present in the hotel safe, but she would much rather keep it here to look at and gloat over, for a while, anyway.

When the knock at the door came, Miranda jumped. She hastily replaced her present in its box, on top of the documents, and pushed the box to one side on the dressing-table, so that it was partly obscured by the bottle of Haig she still had out and by Wilberforce, who looked more bedraggled than ever.

'Come in,' she called. Her visitor did.

'Hello there,' he said, treating her to a sweeter smile than she'd seen on his face before. 'I thought it was about time I got to know you a bit better— and vice versa.' He perched on the edge of her bed and his eyes lit on the bottle of Haig. 'That looks as welcome as an oasis in the desert. Now, if you were to offer me some, with water, and have one yourself, not only would it oil the wheels of conversation, so to speak, but I'd even buy you a new bottle. Scout's honour.'

Miranda, prepared for a few moments to throw him out, changed her mind. After all, she'd nothing much to do before dinner except listen to her Sony Walkman and read magazines. Furthermore, though she supposed she shouldn't, she was dying to show off her latest acquisition. Which, after all, she thought, was what Guido would have wanted her to do.

She went into the bathroom and came out with a glass and a plastic mug (intended to hold toothbrushes). Crossing over to the dressing-table she poured a generous measure of Haig into the water in both. She handed him the glass, and held up the mug in front of her face.

'Cheers,' she said, and drank.

'Cheers,' he said, sipping and watching her closely.

SIX

Dee

BELLA ENJOYED going walkies with us. It's not that she doesn't get any exercise at home, but she's trotted her way round the Woodfield parks *ad nauseam* and animals enjoy a change of scene as much as humans. Mind you, by the time we'd gone down several lanes, lost Fifi and found her again, and passed the time of day with a nice young fair-haired policeman who was wheeling a bicycle along, we were getting a bit tired of fresh air.

When I say 'we' I mean Joyce Bradley and myself, who had opted for exercise and the Sussex countryside, which in spite of the rapidly-vanishing December sun was looking picturesque.

Joyce, who had been looking a bit down, cheered up rapidly during our walk, and in the intervals of calling a lolloping Ajax to heel, even volunteered some information about herself and the beautiful young man who accompanied her at The Grove. She was fairly reticent, but reading between the lines one detected a massive insecurity which the Angel Gabriel wasn't helping overmuch. I decided she was nice, and on further acquaintance would probably prove an interesting person, however convinced she was that she was the reverse.

When we got back and redelivered the dogs (me giving Bella a parting kiss on her wet little nose) I was none too enchanted to find that *La* bloody *Primavera* had commandeered the entire male contingent for croquet, including my old man, but, as I remarked airily to Joyce, 'there's safety in numbers'. Not that I distrust Barry, but he does have this weak spot for feminine pulchritude and girls do seem to like flirting with him. I like a harmless little flirt myself, so I can understand it; nevertheless one doesn't like to feel that one's presence has probably gone totally unmissed by anyone.

Joyce just looked miserable, and I declared, 'Oh, to hell with it, I want to get out of the hotel anyway. What do you say we skip off to Rye for lunch and have a walkabout?'

Rather to my surprise, Joyce agreed, so we were soon bowling merrily away in the car.

Once arrived, I suggested a drink in the famous Mermaid Inn, and after we had toiled up cobbled streets to its half-timbered glories we were able to sip brandies (I insisted on brandy, as giving the authentic feel—we could pretend it had been smuggled by the Hawkhurst gang) under the aloof gaze of Philip of Spain, looking out rather vaguely from his canvas. On the way back from the Ladies I spotted, with astonishment, a figure that I recognized, and while Joyce went to take her turn I plonked myself down at his table and introduced myself.

'You're Morgan Grant, aren't you? My husband bought me one of your pictures—in Florence. A study of the Ponte Vecchio. We like it very much.'

Well, there aren't many people who wear swirling black capes and swirling black locks (the hat, for some reason, was absent) and who look like Richard III on a good day. Actually, Morgan blended in with the environment very well—I daresay some of the literati and artists who had gathered here in the nineteenth and early twentieth centuries would have welcomed him without turning a hair.

By the time Joyce had returned from the queue in the loo we were quite pally—I'd told him about Barry's *Framed Murder* and he'd given me his London address in case he could help or in case we ever decided to invest in one of his *oeuvres* again. He said he was having 'a few days peace and quiet' at a B&B in Rye, and when I mentioned Barry and I were staying at The Grove there was a slight start.

Oho, thought I, so the 'few days peace and quiet are not unconnected with the fair Miranda'. I wondered if he intended to turn up at the hotel, but hadn't got up the nerve yet.

Since Joyce returned at that moment and I had no wish to launch into pointless introductions, I made my adieux, paid for the brandies, and guided the by-now-curious Joyce to the door.

It was beginning to look a bit drizzly, and the brandies had stirred our appetites, so after a bit of desultory wandering along picturesque alleys and peering in picturesque antique shops and art galleries we made our way down to the lower level of the town and lunched munificently at one of the various restaurants specializing in seafoods which Rye boasts. Joyce stuck to Lemon Sole but I had 'Salmon Poached in a Court-Bouillon with a White Wine and Dill Sauce'—and certainly didn't regret it. Over dessert and coffee I explained about Morgan Grant and how we had encountered him (and Miranda) in Florence. Joyce's normally friendly face turned quite white and pinched and wore an expression as near vicious as I guessed one would ever see on it.

'I feel sorry for him, I really do. That girl—she's nothing but trouble. She's got to string along any man she sees, just to satisfy her monumental ego. And of course she's got Gabe wound round her lacquered little finger by now. I honestly think he forgot all about my existence today. Why can't she leave him alone, Dee? From what you said she goes for the rich and famous ultra-talented. Gabe's bright, and good-looking of course, and he can be very charming at times, but he's not in that class at all.'

'Charm and good looks and personality have their own very potent attraction, you know,' I pointed out gently.

'Oh, *don't* I know.' Joyce crumbled a bread roll distractedly. 'I know if it wasn't her it would be someone else. But there have been—other people—and we've survived it. But Miranda—it's as if she's a kind of witch, or something. I mean, Gabriel's not that much of a pushover for beauty. He's so handsome himself that I don't think he notices beautiful people the way most of us do. But she's got him hooked with the matey-matey, let's all have fun together line, and gradually he's getting closer to her, or so he thinks, anyway. One of these days—or hours—he'll suddenly realize she's a knockout as well, and, hey presto...'

'But Joyce, this is all surmise,' I said. 'I mean, you've built up this big scenario in your mind, and it's partly imaginary, surely.'

But Joyce shook her head stubbornly. 'It isn't, Dee. You see, I've seen it happen before, once, with a girl rather like Miranda. Pretty, rich bitch.'

'I don't think Miranda's that rich,' I objected.

'But she will be. She's part chorus-girl type and part socialite and part graduate new-woman. That kind has all the strengths of each type and the combination's formidable.'

'You seem to know a lot about her,' I said, rather surprised by this in-depth analysis.

'Oh, I read magazine and newspaper articles. When she wafted in with her luggage and her virgin-snow outfit, I smelt trouble as well as expensive scent.'

'What happened—with that other girl?' I asked cautiously. 'If you don't mind me asking, that is.'

Joyce gulped down some coffee and her face hardened still further. 'Gabe went off with her. For a weekend at first, then for another, and another, and finally for always, as he thought. She ditched him within a week and since he wouldn't come grovelling, I had to go and search him out. *Not* the best thing for one's pride.' She saw the expression on my face before I had time to change it and added, 'Oh, I know what you're thinking. I'd be better off without him, and all that. Well, maybe I would. But we complement each other, Dee, and he's happy with me. It's one kind of love. If we split up, well, I'm not saying I'd die without him, because I wouldn't. I'm just saying I'd find it damned hard to pick up the pieces, that's all.'

As we waited for the waitress to bring the bill, I strove for a lighter note.

'Let's go and look at the Landgate. And Turkey-cock Lane. There's a legend about a monk and a girl and Turkey-cock Lane. I'll tell you as we go along.'

As we waited for our change, Joyce had her final say about Miranda.

'I know it's very wrong to hate someone, Dee, but I'm afraid I hate Miranda already. You see, I think she's a sort of force, bringing the beginning of the end for Gabe and me. I could murder her. I wish someone would!'

It's the kind of remark people frequently make, but it produces an awkward silence. I chattered brightly on as we wandered our way round part of Rye, and by the time we'd admired the Quarter Boys striking the quarter-hour at St Mary the Virgin, we were ready for more refreshment at Simon the Pieman's.

'Did you know,' I asked, 'that the locals call the little lanes here "twitterings". I think that's lovely.'

'No, I didn't, and yes, it is.' Joyce looked amused. 'You ought to be the teacher, Dee, not I. How come you know all these quaint facts? That one isn't in the guide book.'

'It comes from my husband being a historian,' I explained. 'You've no idea the odd facts I pick up in the course of a marriage!' Joyce laughed again, and Miranda Travers was not, to my relief, mentioned again.

AS WE TURNED into the driveway of The Grove a lurking figure stepped out. It was Gabriel. His face lit up when he saw Joyce.

'You *have* been a long time,' he said, a bit reproachfully. 'Why didn't you take me?'

There was an answer to that one, but Joyce didn't make it. As Gabe linked his arm companionably in hers, she turned to me.

'Thanks for the company, Dee. Much more amusing than this *enfant terrible* here.'

I loitered, pretending acute interest in shrubs, till they had vanished into the house—I know when I'm *de trop*—and in fact, I even wandered back into the roadway again.

Which was how I saw the Santa before anyone else did. He was wearing an oilskin and matching hat, so he didn't at first stand out any more than any other motor-bike rider as he came zooming along the road. When he came to an unsteady halt, however, and whipped off the oilskins, I blinked.

'Hey, Miss,' he called. I looked around to see if there was anyone else littering the roadway who might answer to the description of 'Hey, Miss.' There wasn't. Obligingly, I trotted over. We Vaughans are glad to be of service, especially to Santa Claus.

The drizzle was getting to his white hair and beard and white bushy eyebrows, one of which seemed to be attached precariously to its moorings. Under the trappings his face, rather than being red and jolly, was smooth and olive-skinned, with the kind of big brown eyes one sees in Murillo paintings. And when he spoke again, it was in muted Cockney with slight sing-song underlay. Latin-type, I decided, from Inner London somewhere. Possibly Soho, or Clerkenwell.

'Is that The Grove?' He gestured towards the ho-tel—a full-blooded gesture, like Pavarotti giving his all in *Rigoletto* or *Tosca*. I suppose he just wanted to make sure, but it was, after all, the only sizeable Georgian pile around. The *only* Georgian pile, in fact.

'Certainly it is. I'm staying there. Can I help you?'

He scratched his white Santa wig. I guess it got hot under there.

'Well, it's like this, see. I've got this commis-sion, that is, the firm, Santagrams Ltd have, but it's my special responsibility seeing it's from Mr Mon-tefalcone, and he's real important and he'll have my guts for garters if it doesn't get into the right hands. 'Cause it's very valuable—like priceless, see.'

Allowing for exaggeration, I did. I was intrigued. No prizes for guessing who the priceless object was destined for, and Santa confirmed this a moment later.

'Oh, that's all right. She's staying at the hotel, all right, and I imagine she's there at this minute. Reception will give her a buzz and you can hand

the thingie over to her and go on your way rejoic-
ing.'

'That's OK then.'

He was just revving up the Honda again when I
asked, not with any real hope of being told, 'What
are you delivering, anyway?'

Santa stopped in mid-rev and dug into his
satchel. With infinite care he drew out a parcel. It
was like any other parcel.

'I mean, what's in it?'

I waited for him to tell me to get stuffed, but to
my surprise, after a measuring look, he spilled the
goods.

'Statue. *Little* statue,' he added, as my eyebrows
rose. 'Very beautiful. Made by a famous Italian
craftsman. Very famous. Very, very old.'

I followed the Honda at a sedate pace, wondering
whether 'very, very old' referred to the 'little
statue' or to the Italian craftsman—or both—and
was in time to witness the presentation ceremony
by the Reception desk. Which was pure comic
opera. *Tosca* no, *Figaro* perhaps.

La Travers wafted off, presumably to her boudoir
to examine the spoils in gleeful peace, and Santa
roared away on the red Honda, mission accom-
plished and his guts intact.

I went in search of Barry, and found him
stretched out asleep, covered with pages of the
Framed Murder manuscript which rose and fell

gently as he breathed. I moved the pages to the escritoire, noting disapprovingly that he appeared only to be at page fifty, which to my mind did not constitute 'nearly finished', and covered him with the quilt. I then kicked off shoes and shrugged off outer garments and curled up in the twin bed with one of my paperbacks. That would keep me going till the pre-dinner bath and dress ritual. In fact, I fell asleep too—all that Sussex air.

Barry

IT WAS Christmas Eve. I had spent part of the previous afternoon asleep, and dinner passed unremarkably, except for the Kentish lamb on the menu, which was delicious. I noted that the Major, Joyce and Gabriel were dining in a threesome, and that the Major was being specially attentive to Joyce. Gabriel didn't seem too happy about the Major's old-world courtesy being switched on to Ms Bradley.

Later, in the bedroom, Dee filled me in on her exciting day, and we both agonised with curiosity over Miranda's mysterious parcel.

'I expect she's put it in the hotel safe by now,' I said. 'So it's no good trying to sneak a look. I

mean, she'd hardly get it out again just to show
us.'

Dee agreed, regretfully, that that was unlikely.
'Though she might for you, darling,' she said
sweetly, 'seeing that you get on so well with her—
you and the other 75% of the male population
round these parts.'

I blushed and contested this, but Dee was not
convinced.

'Anyway, I wouldn't say the Major gets on that
well with her—he's just polite to all women on
principle.'

'Well, he's a bit old for her,' Dee agreed. 'I was
glad to see him making a bit of a play for Joyce
Bradley at dinner, though. Show Gabriel that he's
not the only pebble on the beach. She's really got
it bad for him.'

'I suppose you've been doing the girlish confidences bit again,' I teased.

Dee didn't deny it. She filled me in on the afternoon's conversation. 'If you ask me, the girl
seems totally neurotic and obsessed and young
Field would be as well off without her as she would
without him,' I observed crisply. Dee giggled, and
I raised a pained eyebrow.

'I wasn't aware of saying anything particularly
funny.'

'It's just the way you said "young Field." Like
one of those headmaster or lieutenant-colonel

types. Darling, you're still young and sexy, you know.'

'As the delectable Miranda Travers noticed,' I agreed, and got a pillow thrown at me.

'Funny, though,' Dee remarked thoughtfully after the ensuing tussle. 'Joyce is obviously prejudiced against Miranda because of her experience involving Gabe with this other girl. And she is remarkably virulent about Miranda, considering that, as far as we know, all they've done is spend some time together perfectly innocently. Her middle-aged complex, maybe. But when she said she wished someone would murder Miranda, I felt really uncomfortable, as if someone walked over my grave. Maybe someone will, sometime. A thwarted suitor or a jealous rival.'

'As long as they don't do it this Christmas,' I said facetiously. 'We're here for a rest, remember?'

'One of us is. The other is supposed to be working on *Framed Murder*. And who said he'd nearly finished? When I looked you'd only got as far as page fifty. I bet no one's even been murdered yet!'

'Well, I'm stuck.' I felt defensive and sounded it. It's no joke being expected to produce spoofy thrillers at the drop of a hat, as well as grappling with the new syllabus and the Machiavellian politics at Woodfield Tech. I'd like to see Dee trying it.

'Poor lamb. Maybe we could go and have a rootle round Anthony Avery's antique shop, or descend on Morgan Grant for inspiration. He's here, by the way.'

'Who? Morgan Grant?' I must have looked suitably startled. 'I haven't seen him.'

'Not at The Grove, *dumkopf.* In Rye. At a B&B. I encountered him sunk in Byronic thought and double whiskies at The Mermaid. Of course he *might* turn up here at any moment. Not that he'd have much hope with *La Primavera* after caro Guido's little Santagram.'

DEE IS GOOD AT inspired guesses. The day of 24 December was spent mainly *en famille,* so to speak. That is, me, Dee and Bella, whom we rescued from her quarters, took for walkies and brought into Rye with us.

As we left the hotel we saw a cyclist wending his weary way towards it. The phenomenally bright weather we had been having had by now given place to a drear chill which was more in keeping with the time of year, but he must have been warm enough in his cape and muffler. The flamboyant black hat was replaced by a woolly multi-coloured pull-on cap with a bobble, from which his dark locks spilt incongruously.

'Ah, love,' sighed Dee. 'Would you cycle miles to court me, Barry?'

'No need. I've got you now.'

'Well, if you hadn't?'

'Certainly,' I replied promptly. Always tell women what they want to hear, when there is no fear of them taking you up on it. I spoilt the effect, however, by adding truthfully, 'I'd prefer the Mini, though.' Dee ignored this.

'Suitor number two,' she said thoughtfully. 'I wonder if Robert Thornton will turn up.'

'If he does, it will be in a custom-built limo, with a fanfare of trumpets. Anyway, Guido Doo-da isn't *en scène,* is he?'

'No, but his present is. I'm beginning to feel a bit sorry for Miranda. I mean, she's kind of hemmed in on all sides, isn't she?'

'Enough to make a girl enter a nunnery,' I agreed.

Dee gave me a push, and Bella joined in the horseplay, licking my face enthusiastically, till Dee hauled her off.

'Barry washed his face this morning, Bella. He doesn't need your efforts. He's a clean boy.'

Bella wagged her tail—her sense of humour is developed, as of course it would be, *chez* Vaughan.

I enjoyed the cobbled and half-timbered picturesqueness of Rye; I knew the town already, but it's always worth another visit. Bella was very little trouble, and kept pretty closely to heel, her stubby tail wagging periodically. It was easy to imagine the smugglers coming in from Romney in a misty dawn and old Henry James taking mulled punch on frosty December days while he planned out another tale. I wondered what he would have made of a Miranda.

Some shops were still open for the Christmas Eve rush, and we had a superb seafood lunch. Before leaving we managed to locate Avery Antiques, which was in an alley off the High Street. It made up for a slightly inconvenient location (if you didn't know it was there, you would miss it) by a wide frontage and a well-chosen display.

A large and beautiful Persian carpet covered most of the floor area, and in the centre was a fine Regency mahogany three-pedestal dining table and matching chairs, set for dinner, with a branched silver candelabrum in the centre. The other items of furniture—a bureau bookcase, a serpentine mahogany sideboard, and circular tripod tables—were Georgian or Regency. Dee pointed out a girandole mirror, which she thought was maybe Louis XIV, and the odd *objet d'art* which was tastefully displayed on top of the sideboard and tables—such as a jade horse, a Worcester bowl with fruit in it, and a graceful Attic amphora, with black figures on a pale ground.

The general effect was understatement, and there was no doubt that Anthony Avery Antiques was not for the browser with an odd fifty or so to spend on some little toy that caught his or her fancy. Even the very cheapest of the small items would set you back at least £500. Not for the millionaire, but for the well-heeled eclectic buyer. I was rather glad the notice said 'Closed' as Dee's nostrils were quivering as she looked at the *objets,* in rather the same way that Bella's did when she looked at her bowl of Chunky Morsels.

'You're after an item of furniture, remember,' I told her sternly. 'Not Greek vases and Chinese horses.'

'Well, a girl can look, can't she?'

'As long as it's just looking. Never mind the quality, think of the price-tag.'

I decided then and there that if Dee paid another visit to Avery Antiques before we left Sussex then I'd tag along with her. Just as a restraining force, you understand. Husbands of the world, unite!

Bella, as if she sensed the direction of my thoughts, growled. Well, she is a female. And, come to think of it, *she* is one of Dee's little extravagances, though a welcome one.

Back at the old homestead, fun and games were in progress when we walked in. Literally. The Major and Terence Fitzgerald had rounded up everyone else, card and board games were littered around the drawing-room, and a rowdy game of Pass-the-Parcel was going on. Joyce was laughing and flushed and mine host and hostess had joined the merry throng.

Other equally rowdy romps followed, with Dee and myself throwing ourselves into the spirit of the thing. Musical Chairs round the dining-room, with Joyce belting out on the piano there, proved a great success; and when we got tired of that, the Major led a good old knees-up, with the old music-hall favourites.

'You've really got everyone going,' I remarked admiringly to him, in between 'Lily of Laguna' and 'Don't Dilly-Dally on the Road'.

He looked pleased. 'Well, if somebody doesn't, everyone will just eat and wander round and watch the telly all the time. Leading to indigestion, quarrels and what-have-you.' He didn't mention the words *esprit de corps* or *noblesse oblige,* but I felt like standing to attention and saluting.

'Anyway, I enjoy it. Brings back the old family Christmas.' He looked, briefly, sad, then threw himself into the next chorus with gusto. A nice old guy. Another couple of decades and his type would be extinct. Pity.

After dinner we drifted back into the drawing-room. No one wanted to watch the telly and with the exception of Anthony Avery, who wore an expression of coolly amused detachment, everyone seemed eager to maintain the party spirit. Even Miranda, in black velvet trouser suit, white ruffled shirt and black Alice band, was more like an extrovert teenager than the cool young madam she normally presented to the world, as she swapped jokes with Terence Fitzgerald, giggling and pushing him around.

I forgot to say that Morgan Grant had joined the hotel guests—apparently, as Dee found out by the simple expedient of asking him, the Brewers had agreed to let him stay the night in one of the unoccupied rooms on the top floor, and the Major had offered a spare pair of pyjamas, he and Morgan being much of a size.

Morgan had joined in very well up to now, and had revealed a surprisingly good baritone voice in the sing-song, but now he looked stormy. Dee hastily collared him, and led him off to a corner. Anthony Avery had looked disapproving, also, and I wondered briefly what his relationship was with Terence. Perhaps he was gay and Terence wasn't. Or more likely, he disapproved of Miranda, full stop, and had no wish to see his friend and business partner becoming entwined in her Circean toils.

Charades came next, and Bella was roped in as a prop, but banished after she became over-excited and nipped Anthony Avery's ankle—at least, that's how Dee excused her, but I suspect that Bella just took a dislike to Anthony. Well, he had tweaked her tail, which she loathes, and had referred to her patronisingly as 'the pooch' to boot. I don't blame Bella—no mere pooch she, but a highly intelligent

Schnauzer. I'm sure Crufts would greet her with cries of joy, if we went in for that kind of thing.

'Oh, let her stay,' pleaded Miranda. 'You won't do it again, will you, Bella?'

'Uuurgh-humph,' Bella replied, woolly coat a-bristle. It was a non-committal answer, and Dee settled the question by bearing Bella off to rejoin Ajax and Fifi, who had clearly been missing her. Harmony was restored.

It was a pity that in the next charade, in the third scene, Gabriel Field should have been the one to kiss Miranda under the mistletoe. And even more of a pity that he should have done so with enjoyment. I shot a glance at Joyce Bradley, who was trying to look unconcerned, without success. Her attempt at a smile was more like a snarl. Dee's eyes met mine, and she rushed in to cover the awkwardness sensed by everyone.

'Mistletoe, of course! It's obvious. But I think missal, as in prayerbook, was tough...'

'What else could you have?' objected Miranda. 'Missel as in missel-thrush? That's just as obscure.'

'Mistletoe. A parasite growing on the trunks of trees. The berries are poisonous to man. Used as a ceremonial plant in the past, a long way back. That may be why we use it for decoration at Christmas.'

'So why do people kiss under it?' Miranda was looking interested and my diversionary tactics had just led back to the awkwardness.

'Who knows? Dee, you guessed it first, so your team had better think up a good one.'

Conversation became general as Dee's team went out of the room, and mistletoe and kissing were forgotten. Though the Major did murmur to me, 'That girl's riding for a fall. No tact. I wouldn't be surprised if something really bad happens to her one of these days. Not,' he added hastily, 'that one wants it to. But she does need a lesson.' Harsh words, for the Major.

Dee's team didn't succeed in fooling us either, and since the evening was now well advanced, Murder in the Dark won the most votes as final game. I think Morgan suggested it, but then, it was an obvious choice, scary games being popular with both children and adults, like ghost stories.

We'd played a couple of times and were on the third round when I slipped out of the room. By this time, hours of unremitting jollity were beginning to grate on me, and I felt I wanted a few minutes on my own. Besides, I had just had an inspiration for the current opus, and needed some peace and quiet to think it out. I didn't disappear altogether, as I had a feeling the party was going to break up pretty soon anyway.

The door opened and shut again quickly, and someone slipped out shortly after me. The light wasn't on, but I could make out a figure leaning against the wall. It was breathing quickly and distressfully, and I heard the breath catch in a sob. Even if it hadn't been for its size and the glint of pale hair, it would still have been easy to identify Miranda Travers from the delicate wave of 'Eau de Rochas' which wafted from her.

I moved towards Miranda and cleared my throat, just to make sure she knew someone was there. She started, and a frightened voice hissed, 'Who is it?'

'Just me,' I said apologetically. 'Barry Vaughan.' I sensed as well as heard the relieved expulsion of breath, and she moved towards me. A hand rested on my sleeve.

'I'm frightened,' she said simply. I patted the hand vaguely and made a sort of soothing noise.

Then I asked, equally simply, 'Why?'

'Because during the last game, when it was all dark, someone came up behind me and put something round my neck and twisted it tight and pulled. And a voice whispered "You're going to die, Miranda."' She shuddered. 'It was horrible. Just like one of those scary Hitchcock films. I knew I wasn't the "body" in that game because I'd overheard who it was before that. It was Joyce, and I couldn't have been mistaken for Joyce in the dark, because whoever it was said my name. I don't know if it was a man or a woman—you know, one doesn't, with whispers.'

'How perfectly awful,' I sympathised, thinking I now sounded rather like a prefect of the Upper

Sixth, rather than a headmaster. But Miranda Travers and her proximity made me feel distinctly nervous.

'Don't you think, though, it was just someone playing a joke in bad taste? I mean, off-putting, but not to be taken seriously.'

'Maybe.' Miranda did not sound convinced. 'It sounded threatening to me. I know what it was round my neck, too—at least I'm fairly sure. Morgan's woolly muffler. But I don't think it was Morgan—it's not his style at all. I don't *know*, of course.'

That's the point. It's the *not knowing* that makes experiences like this frightening. All the same, I was still inclined to put the whole thing down to a bad joke. Certainly not worth a full-scale questioning.

I managed to calm Miranda and after a bit we were chatting desultorily and I was telling her about Woodfield Tech. She seemed interested—or maybe that's the act she puts on for all the male sex. At any rate, when I suggested we go in and join the others, she agreed, and gave me a grateful little hug.

'You're very sane and calm, Barry dear. Just what I need. You're wife's a lucky woman.' Rank and gross flattery, of course, but who's immune to it? Particularly from a pretty girl.

There were one or two raised eyebrows as Miranda and I entered together. The lights were on again and the game had finished. I noticed Morgan Grant's muffler draped carelessly over the back of a chair. He was nowhere near it. Would Morgan have played such a nasty trick on Miranda? Possibly, if she had been teasing him or being generally scathing. Though in that case, would he have agreed to stay the night at The Grove? Surely he'd have pedaled off in high dudgeon to his B&B.

Suddenly from the entrance part of the hotel there came the faint sound of voices raised in song. We trooped out, and Mrs. Brewer flung the door wide to a burst of 'Hark, the Herald Angels Sing'. We gave quite generously into their collecting tin after a jolly 'Good King Wenceslas' and a spiritual 'Silent Night, Holy Night', which always makes Dee tearful—she says it's so beautiful it gets her tear ducts going.

The Brewers invited the carol singers in for cocoa or a hot toddy, but they refused, saying they had several houses to visit yet, and scrunched their way up the gravel path, torches bobbing, to a chorus of 'Merry Christmas!' And after that it was bed for all.

CHRISTMAS MORNING, and Dee and I exchanged presents. I got a cream Arran sweater, a biography of Disraeli and another of Elizabeth I (both the latest out) and a big hug. Dee got a cassette of Elkie

Brooks and another of Carly Simon, an Arden lipstick, two detective novels by favourite Collins Crime Club authors and a cheque for £400 to put towards an *objet d'art* or whatever. She got a hug too. Dee said the cheque was generous. I agreed. Bella got a new drinking bowl, a rubber ball and a promissory note for many tins of Chunky Morsels and some genuine liver, steak and chicken. There isn't much in the intellectual line one can get for a dog. Maybe she'll enjoy listening to Dee's tapes.

We then made off for church. The other occupants of The Grove were either asleep or similarly engaged. The day passed somnolently and satisfyingly, like most Christmas Days. Lots of eating and drinking, crackers and paper hats, telly, more telly and yet more telly. On the whole, I felt, it was not going to be a memorable Christmas.

MIRANDA TRAVERS went walking with Morgan Grant. He proposed and she refused. He asked her to think about it and she said she would. Then he returned to Rye on his bike.

Miranda had a couple of phone calls in the course of the day, one of which was from Robert Thornton.

Anthony Avery, bored to tears, decided to miss the plum pud and see to some vital matters at his shop. He set off later than planned, so told the

Brewers he might stay overnight in the flat above the shop.

Terence Fitzgerald made some long-distance calls to Dublin and drank too much.

No one went to bed very early—possibly because they had all eaten and drunk too much to have the energy to get up the stairs.

In the early hours of the morning of Boxing Day an event occurred which had almost certainly never occurred before at The Grove. At least, not in the twentieth century.

SEVEN

Dee

I CAN'T SAY it was the most peaceful of nights. Everyone in the place had retired by midnight, but at 1.15 or so we were woken by a loud noise, which was repeated...and repeated...and repeated. Bella started barking and I had to shut her up, while Barry pulled on his dressing-gown and went to investigate. At first I'd thought it was a burglar alarm—then I realised what it was: a digital alarm, the same as we had on our room radio, which just hadn't been switched off.

I poked my head round the door of the room, and saw the Major emerging from number nine and a tousled Terry Fitzgerald, swearing poetically, from number eleven. The fair Miranda in number thirteen was either sleeping the sleep of the just, or lying doggo and hoping the sound would go away—which was exactly what Barry and I had done, for the first couple of minutes.

'Jaysus,' declaimed Terry, after giving a thump to the door of number twelve, 'will you stop that racket now.'

Major Gardner coughed. 'Since this is Mr Avery's room and since I understand Mr Avery is spending the night at his flat in Rye, I imagine the only way to stop the alarm is to get in.'

'Which would mean rousing the Brewers, who are in their staff flat,' added Barry, who had already tried the door of number twelve to no avail.

Barry and the Major set off down the stairs and Terry bumbled and grumbled round. He was looking rather fetching in a wool Kaftan in dark stripes, a bit Wise-Man-of-the-East-ish, except for his hair sticking up in a parrot-like crest, and his Hibernian turn of phrase.

'You'd better go back to bed, Terry,' I said. 'I can hear them coming back now, and there's nothing either of us can do.'

'Woof,' agreed Bella, who had sidled to the door and stuck her muzzle out. Her tail was wagging hopefully. Midnight feasties?

I went back to bed myself and after a while the irritating high-pitched beeping stopped, leaving what seemed like an almost tangible silence in comparison, and Barry returned and climbed into bed. Bella cocked one ear, opened one eye, looked at him and grunted.

'I take it Robin switched the thing off,' I ventured.

'You take it right.' Barry was not at his best. He dislikes being woken from his slumbers for anything on a smaller scale than the Massacre of the Innocents. 'Bloody thoughtless of Avery,' he muttered on. 'And why anyone would want to suddenly whizz off to Rye on Christmas Night of all times…seems bloody fishy to me.'

I agreed that I thought it highly unlikely that anyone would choose that particular time suddenly to start stocktaking or checking a delivery of porcelain or whatever.

'Cherchez la femme?' I suggested.

'Mmmmph.' Barry turned his back and switched off the bedside lamp. He was not, his humped-up form seemed to say, very interested in *femmes* or any other hypotheses to explain eccentric behaviour. Not tonight, anyway.

At about four in the morning I awoke again. I'm not sure if I woke or was woken. Certainly Bella was rampant and growling softly, ears pricked.

I slid out of the bed, which creaked, cast an apprehensive look at Barry, who would *not* appreciate being disturbed again, tiptoed to the door, and cast a cautious glance out into the corridor. Sweet nothing. Quiet as the grave. Not a soul was stirring, not even a mouse. The fact that I felt a chilly sense of unease might well have been due to the fact that I was barefoot and wearing a thin white lawn nightie—or it might have been the Ghost of The Grove reaching me with an eerie sense of its phantom presence.

I hastily abandoned any project of night exploration, shushed Bella, who nevertheless scratched at the door a few times before giving up, and climbed back into bed. I did think I heard a sort of scrunchy sound from below the window, but when I went to investigate I couldn't see anything except weaving shadows, quite ephemeral.

'Sod off,' I muttered to any ghostly presence out there. I'm not more cowardly than the normal person, but this was the second time that night, and enough is enough.

Both Bella and I slept fitfully after that, and when she roused me for walkies at six-fifteen, I bowed to the inevitable. Not only was I peckish (and I vaguely remembered a bowl of crisps and another of nuts and raisins lurking near the Christmas cards in the drawing-room) but I had also left my new Elizabeth Ferrars hardback by the side of an armchair. Since Barry, if up to his usual Christmas form, would sleep on happily till woken, I might as well recover my read.

'Just as well your bladder problems coincide with my morning starvation, my girl,' I told Bella.

But my little dog showed no inclination to make for the Reception desk, front door and great outdoors beyond. Instead, she made firmly for the drawing-room. She was whining and her mood of anxiety communicated itself to me. Dogs have far more acute hearing than people, and some of them seem to be able to sense things we can't. So I was prepared for *something* of an unpleasant nature as I pushed open the door to the drawing-room.

At first I didn't see it. There was, after all, a sofa blocking the view. But Bella made straight for it, and starting sniffing and whining. I say 'it' but I should have said 'her'. Miranda Travers lay, body twisted but face up, one arm flung out wide. She was wearing a long ivory silk nightdress and a matching negligee trimmed with lace. Very good lace. A small satin and swansdown mule lay on its side near one bare foot. She looked like Ophelia; fragile, pathetic. But there were no flowers. The index finger of the outstretched hand seemed to be pointing directly at my book, lying face-down where I had left it by the armchair. I picked it up. The word 'Murder' in the title leapt out at me.

I knew Miranda was dead, but nevertheless I observed the forms and checked her breathing (non-existent) and her pulse, which as expected did not beat. Her hand felt cold to the touch. Not icy, but cold. Her nightwear would have been highly impractical for icy December if the hotel had not been comfortably centrally heated.

I got up from my knees and my glance was drawn upwards for some reason. There hung the heavy ornate chandelier, with the mistletoe suspended from it, its berries looking sickly and pale. Now it seemed an evil, malevolent symbol, this parasite plant, and I shivered as I recalled those two beautiful people, Gabriel and Miranda, briefly clasped in each other's arms underneath it in the charade the night before.

I became aware that there was a draught—my chill was not due solely to horror—and I walked over to the French window, which appeared to be off the catch. I was about to close it, then stopped. I remembered Bella's unease during the early hours. If there had been an intruder... And in any case everything should be left exactly as it was till the police had been... But why should I have thought 'police'? Surely, 'doctor'. Miranda had not been shot—there was no entry wound and no blood. She had not been garrotted, and she had not been bludgeoned to death. There was no ivory paperknife sticking through her heart, to match the ivory negligee. Unless she had been poisoned, in which case she would surely look far worse than she did, then it must be a natural death, or a drugs overdose or something, though I would have said Miranda was certainly not the type. Too clearheaded and careful of her looks.

Quickly I pushed up the wide sleeves. There appeared to be two small punctures, away from any vein—rather like accidental pricks with something sharp. Definitely not a junkie. There was a faint discolouration round the throat area, but I thought that would be explained by the practical joke with the muffler which Barry had told me about. Some joke!

'You're going to die, Miranda!' And she had. My instincts said 'Murder', as did poor Miranda's finger, pointing at my book. Coincidence, of course. Appearances said not. Now we would have to wait for the doctor.

Bella whined again, and snuffled gently at Miranda's ear. I remembered that though I had not liked the girl, she had made a pet of Bella during the previous day's romps. *De mortuis nil nisi bonum*—everyone has their good points. I was roused from my reverie by Barry's voice.

'Dee—what the hell's happened?'

'Miranda Travers,' I said, 'is dead.' And then, 'You'd better get onto the Brewers, and get them to call a doctor as soon as possible.'

'Nothing, I take it, to be disturbed.'

'Precisely.'

'Poor, pretty Miranda,' he said, compassionately, and was gone.

THE BREWERS took it well, considering. True, I hadn't expected Betty to do a Lady Macbeth and wail 'What, in our house?', and she did seem distressed, to the extent of actually wringing her hands, but practicality prevailed, the drawing-room was locked, and Dr Fry was summoned. His verdict was cardiac arrest.

Even the Brewers blinked a bit at that one, and I protested squeakily, 'Cardiac arrest—at *her* age?'

Dr Fry, who was small, rotund and had 'Family Physician' written all over him, was peeved.

'There may well be a history of heart condition. It's not unknown among young people, you know. I shall have to find that out. If so, a sudden shock, or overexertion may have been enough...'

'You don't think...' Barry began.

'That there was "foul play"?' Dr Fry regarded him drily. He obviously knew of Barry as a crime-story writer, and considered him in the light of one who sees skeletons in every cupboard and corpses in every private hotel. 'Most unlikely.'

Barry enquired, in his sleuth-voice, if there were any external injuries.

'A contusion at the back of the head, which would be explained by her striking her head against the side of a table as she went down. Which, given her position in regard to one of the side tables knocked askew, seems likely.'

I tried to visualise the room and remembered that there had been a table askew.

'You don't think she could have been knocked out by an intruder, this causing both the contusion and the heart attack?'

Dr Fry admitted it was not impossible, though most improbable, his manner stated equally clearly. It was quite obvious that the *corpus delicti*, just a short while ago the beautiful Miranda Travers, was going to be removed, claimed by her family, the funeral arranged, and Cardiac Arrest stated on the death certificate. And anyone who wanted further enquiries into the matter would have to have good reasons and a good deal of influence.

'So what,' I demanded later, 'do we do now? Leave it?'

'Well, after all,' Barry pointed out, 'we haven't got a shred of proof that anything untoward happened. I mean,' he amended, 'foul play.'

'True, but I've got a gut feeling that all is not well, and even if Miranda's heart attack is bona fide, something is rotten in the state of Denmark. We could start looking at the people who might have a reason for wanting Miranda six foot under. I'm sure she was whammed on the head, for a start, and if she did have a dicky heart, that just might have done for her, unlikely as it might seem. And,' I continued, warming to my theme, 'if Robert Thornton doesn't have influence I don't know who has. If he thought his wife-to-be was knocked off, I'm sure he'd persuade Miranda's family to agree and get investigations opened. Even,' I added, 'Scotland Yard.'

'I suppose,' Barry remarked sarcastically, 'in another minute you'll be having Ken Graves walking in to take charge of things.'

'Well, why not, if he's available?' I slid off the

bed I'd been sitting on, cross-legged, and marched purposefully to the door. 'Barry Vaughan, I want you to get your lil ol' notebook, and start figuring out folkses and motives, while I get busy on my own line of investigation.'

'Which is?' my better half demanded.

'Finding out if Miranda put the mysterious Santagift in the hotel safe, and, if so, if it's still there.'

'Something tells me,' Barry grumbled darkly, 'it's back to Nick and Nora time. And I thought this was going to be a quiet holiday!'

'Well, it was—for a while.'

'What about *Framed Murder?*' Barry wailed, as I opened the door.

'Tough shit.' I wasn't sympathetic. Barry, as I knew very well, was 'stuck' and would welcome any excuse to get away from the damned manuscript. Besides, a real live corpse—so to speak—is worth more than an imaginary one, any day. I had enjoyed our bit of sleuthing in the not so dim and distant, when murder and mayhem had been uncovered at Wentworth Hall, in the environs of Woodfield, and Barry and I had found ourselves lending our grey matter to aid the very handsome Detective Inspector Kenneth Graves of the Yard. Ken had later started to see a great deal of my old friend Elizabeth Fane and so *we* had seen something of him, making up the occasional double-date for dinner and a show.

Although obviously I deplored poor Miranda's untimely end, I was itching to get on the sleuthpath again. The letting agency has its hairy moments, but for sheer excitement it certainly can't rival your actual on-the-spot crime.

I managed to find out from Betty Brewer that Miranda had deposited nothing in the hotel safe and I withdrew, thoughtful. Betty had known nothing of the contents of the Santagift, and Katy, who might know a bit more, having been on duty when the thing was delivered, was now on her Christmas break. Since this meant that the Reception desk was left unattended a good part of the time, it was not a difficult task for me to snaffle Miranda's keys and scuttle up the stairs with them. Getting into her room unobserved and quietly was more difficult, but I managed it.

Everything was left as it had been, since the Brewers, like ourselves, thought the safest thing was to lock up the drawing-room and leave things untouched, until we knew whether there was likely to be any investigation or not. A quick look around revealed that Miranda had liked whisky, had cherished a battered toy panda with the name 'Wilberforce' embroidered over his little vest, and that she had used Clarins cosmetics, favoured cut-glass scent-bottles and read glossy mags. It did not reveal any statuette, of a nature valuable or otherwise. A more exhaustive search revealed an earring under the dressing-table, and some exquisite undies in drawers, but no statue.

'WELL,' REMARKED Barry when I had returned the key to its pigeon-hole and made my way thoughtfully back to our room, 'it looks as if your suspicions about the state of Denmark may have been correct. On the other hand, Miranda may have given her present to someone, for safekeeping or valuation, or whatever.'

'Like who?'

'One of the antique dealers, perhaps. She seemed chummy with Terry Fitzgerald.'

'Hmmm.'

'Or Morgan Grant. Miranda would have trusted his judgement, and, I think, him. Also, there's the point that if Miranda had decided to accept Thornton, she might have decided to flog di Montefalcone's present for all the hard cash she could raise, in case he asked for it back. Or even if she decided to give both Thornton and di Montefalcone the brush-off. Morgan might be hanging onto it for her, or Terry. So don't go crying "thief, thief" just yet.'

'I'd find it pretty difficult, anyway. I mean, the fact that I got into Miranda's room pretty easily means anyone else could too, so the *objet* might easily have been nicked. But I can hardly reveal the fact that I sneaked in to take a dekko without making myself a suspicious character. Even a suspect of said nicking.'

'True, my own. Look, I've started making some notes, as you commanded. Here's the upshot.' Barry cleared his throat. I settled myself comfortably on the bed and wished that, like Miranda, I'd had the foresight to bring along some Haig. Or order coffee from room service. Though it hardly seemed fair to lumber any more tasks on poor old Betty Brewer in the circs.

'One: Robert Thornton was spending Christmas near Bosham. A place called Redditch Grange. He'd been on to Miranda to join him for Christmas *en famille* and she refused, preferring to stay here. I learned this during our little heart-to-heart in the corridor during the Murder in the Dark game.'

'Oh, yes,' I said ominously.

Barry ignored me. 'It would have been possible for Thornton to motor over during the night, having arranged an assignation with Miranda by phone to meet him in the drawing-room in the early hours, letting him in the French window. They could have quarrelled and he could have bopped her one, resulting in heart attack. Or he could have told her something that gave her such a shock that she snuffed it, hitting her head on the way down as Dr Fry suggested. Thornton, being an eminent man, panicked and fled.'

'It doesn't sound very convincing.'

'No, but not impossible. Remember, we're not going into the complicated matter of Miranda's heart attack at the moment, just motives and things. OK?'

'OK,' I nodded.

'Two: Morgan Grant, who was staying here on Christmas Eve, and therefore would have known about the Santagift, presumably from Miranda, either had a quarrel with Miranda and came back to bop her one, or came back to make up, and the Thornton scenario is repeated; or he decided that he'd prefer the *objet* and a life without Miranda, whose little foibles had finally worn him down, and nicked it.

'Three: Joyce Bradley, by her own admission to you, feared and disliked Miranda. The two of them may have had some confrontation in the drawing-room, either by chance or by arrangement, and Joyce literally frightened Miranda to death by some means—or bopped her one in a fury and then got frightened and left her there.

'Four: Gabriel Field had a tryst with Miranda in the drawing-room, for purposes of romance/seduction, or *he* had nicked the Santagift and she was persuading him to give it back, with the result that he bopped her one and made off with the *objet*. A variation on this theme is that she and Gabriel were planning to dispose of the Santagift and she promised him a good cut and they were to go off together on part of the proceeds, either for ever, or, more likely, for a short time. Joyce follows Gabriel and listens outside the door and is so furious that she bursts in and bops Miranda one. Gabriel covers up for her. *Or*, Miranda threatens to expose Gabriel for nicking the *objet*, and Joyce bursts in and threatens *her*, and they haven't replaced the Santagift yet. I don't think Joyce would let Gabriel keep it, though I can see her murdering someone who threatened her ewe lamb, or at any rate frightening them, even if murder wasn't intended.

'Five: Terry Fitzgerald nicks the Santagift—perhaps she has handed it to him for valuation. Repeat of Gabriel Field scenario. That's about as far as I've got.'

'*None* of it sounds very convincing,' I complained. 'Your crime novels are much better.'

'Well, the whole thing is pretty weird,' retorted Barry.

'Your main points seem to be that Miranda may have been frightened to death by accident, which is just about possible if she was jumped on in the dark, I suppose, and the person or persons panicked and kept quiet. And that there are two main motive leads—the theft/exposure one and the *crime passionnel* one.'

'Right. And since we're not going to get anywhere by just sitting twiddling our thumbs, and I think that the local police are going to accept Dr

Fry's accident theory without making much effort to look into the why's and wherefore's, I suggest we hop into the Mini and take a trip to Bosham.'

Which we did.

EIGHT

Barry

REDDITCH GRANGE was much as one might have expected a Sussex country home to be. Namely, mellow red brick with creepers, and immaculate lawns with a curving gravel sweep from the wrought-iron gate. There was a Mercedes parked in front of the olde-worlde oak front door—it belonged to Thornton *fils*, I guessed, rather than to the oldies—and the door of an outhouse stood ajar, revealing a handsome cabin cruiser for summer use. A golden labrador sidled round the side of the house and barked challengingly. Bella, who had come along for the ride, woofed back. She may be small, but she's cheeky with it. The labrador wagged his tail.

We parked the Mini a respectful distance from the Merc, rang the bell and announced ourselves to the elderly retainer who appeared. Obviously we looked respectable enough (though Bella earned a doubtful glance) for we were conducted through an entry hall smelling of lavender polish with vases of late chrysanths on polished oak surfaces, into a pleasant chintz-and-cabinets morning-room. A silver-framed photo of a rather regal-looking couple with silver hair, posing against a box hedge with the labrador, regarded us from the top of a piano. Obviously Robert Thornton's parents, looking to the manor born, for all that he had started life as an errand boy at sixteen and she, though distantly related to Lady this and the Honourable that, had launched herself on society from the West End chorus line.

'So that's the founder of Thornton Enterprises,' Dee said—Thornton Enterprises being the foundation stone of the Thornton industrial empire. 'Looks a fairly formidable old bird. Wonder how he'd have taken to our Miranda—had the nuptials taken place, I mean.'

'Like a house on fire, probably. Remind him of his own wife when she was young, no doubt.' Dee peered sceptically at the framed Lady Thornton— Sir Richard had been knighted a few summers ago for his services to industry.

'I can't imagine Miranda growing into *that*. The mind boggles.'

'You'd be surprised how people adapt,' I said. 'Take me, for instance, caught in the coils of matrimony. Do you hear me sighing for my bachelor days?'

'Frequently, when you have to empty the dustbin.' Dee favoured me with a horrid grimace, sticking her tongue out and wiggling her hands in a yah-boo gesture. Naturally, this was the cue for Robert Thornton to walk in. He looked mildly startled but I suppose it helped to break the ice.

In fact, as might have been expected of such a dynamic type, Robert Thornton was more *au courant* with what was going on than we were. In the time it had taken us to drive over from East Sussex the local police had been put on the job and Mr and Mrs Travers had had the demise of their daughter broken to them. They had decided against driving from the Midlands for the present, since they had been assured there was nothing they could do and Miranda's body was not yet available for interment.

'We feel,' I explained, 'that there's more than meets the eye with Miranda's death, and that it should be looked into further. And with all due respect to the Sussex police...'

'You mean you think Miranda was murdered and you want me to ring the Chief Constable and pull strings to get Scotland Yard in on the act?' If not noticeably angry, Thornton was crisp and certainly pulled no punches.

'Well—yes.' If this was a sample of the incisive action that had got Robert Thornton where he was today (not discounting the help of Sir Richard) then I could only admire it. Unfortunately, working at Woodfield Tech encourages one to become adept in euphemism, hyperbole, double-think, double-talk and filling in forms. But the nitty has lost its gritty long before anyone actually gets round to making a move. True, we'd made a fairly speedy move that morning, but here I was indulging in euphemism etc, for all the world as if I were still pacing the corridors of the Tech and pondering on the next departmental meeting.

'I suppose, Mr Thornton, you're wondering why we should have such a weird suspicion, and are we sensation-mongers or potty or what.' Dee had decided to shove her oar in as I floundered in embarrassment. 'Well, we may not have much to go on but instinct, but my instincts when I found Miranda, for a start—and I was the one who discovered her dead—told me there was something very wrong about her death. And my little dog, Bella, woke me up in the early hours. She was in a disturbed state and wanted to go downstairs. In the morning she led me straight to the drawing-room. I can't help feeling that if I'd followed her the first time instead of shutting her up and going back to sleep, I might have been able to prevent—well, whatever it was that did happen.'

Robert Thornton looked at Dee ironically. For a man whose fiancée—or near-fiancée—had just died, he seemed remarkably in control of his feelings. Or perhaps he just was a very controlled person. His eyes were a cool grey-blue, and at that moment the expression in them was sardonic in the extreme.

'Forgive me if I offend you, Mrs Vaughan, but I can hardly be expected to pull out the stops to get the death of my fiancée investigated just because you have "instincts" and so does your dog. After all, Miranda had a heart condition. Premature though her death was, it seems to have been natural. There is absolutely no evidence to the contrary. And after all, you are strangers, who barely knew Miranda. Be assured that if I felt there was *anything* untoward about her death, I would do all I could to bring it to light.'

Dee persisted. 'A lot of deaths appear to have "nothing untoward" about them. It's only afterwards, when someone raises questions, that there proves to have been something very untoward indeed. OK—you say that if you were sure there was something wrong, you'd do all you could to bring it to light. Now my husband and I barely knew Miranda Travers, as you point out. Also, frankly, from the little I did see of her I did not particularly care for her. She was the kind of person who treads on toes and makes at least some enemies. But I do care about justice. Miranda should not have died. Maybe it was a natural death. If so, we'll feel fools and you'd have stirred up trouble for nothing. But don't you think that that's better than allowing a possible murderer to get away with it? If you'll just

listen to us for a little longer, I think we can convince you that there were a few people with some
kind of a motive for hating Miranda, resenting her
or wanting something she had. And from there to
doing something about it is only a few steps. There
was also opportunity. Even you yourself, Mr
Thornton, are not totally immune from suspicion.'

That's torn it, I thought. We'll be shown the door
any minute now! But Robert Thornton, after a brief
angry thundercloud passing over his face, suddenly
and unexpectedly smiled.

'You've won your point, Mrs Vaughan. I'll listen
to whatever else you have to say. And—may I offer
you tea, coffee? Sandwiches?'

'Yes, *please,*' Dee said gratefully. We'd stopped
for a snack en route, but it hadn't stayed the pangs.
The cold December nip made us hungrier, and now
that I glanced out of the window I could see that
the earlier glint of sun had disappeared and it was
grey and lowering. Possibly snow was in the offing.

'Right, Barry,' Dee declared, when the refreshments had been polished off. 'Over to you.'

I wiped my buttery fingers and fished my notebook out. This had better be convincing, I told myself. Apart from poor Miranda's claims, the honour
of the Vaughans was at stake.

I went over the points Dee and I had made before, with some embellishments. It was a bit awkward explaining the Santagift, but it transpired that

Robert Thornton was well aware of the existence of his romantic Italian rival, and shared our view that the statuette, whatever it was, was probably of value—enough to tempt someone with the requisite knowledge to steal it. Or even someone without the requisite knowledge—after all, there was no knowing to whom Miranda might have spilt the beans. Gabriel Field, for one. Or Terence Fitzgerald. Or even Major Hal Gardner, though this was perhaps unlikely.

'Of course, I would have made Miranda give the statuette back,' Thornton said. 'After all, as my fiancée she could hardly keep a valuable present from another admirer. Something small, perhaps.'

He sounded very sure of himself. Dee and I exchanged a glance.

'But if I am correct, Miranda was *not* your fiancée,' Dee pointed out. 'In fact, she seemed to be hesitating between the two of you.' And the Santagift may well have tipped the scale, her silence added.

Robert Thornton gave a small triumphant smile. 'Yes, we were the two main contenders. In fact, I'm not arrogant enough to accept that di Montefalcone might even have been leading by a short head. But—to keep to the racing metaphor—I pipped him at the post. On Christmas Day I proposed to Miranda by phone, and she accepted. So you see, we were, unofficially, engaged.'

'Oh,' I said. There didn't seem much more *to* say. One could hardly, after all, say congratulations to a man whose newly-acquired fiancée no longer existed. Especially as one has spent the past half hour urging him that she may have been murdered. But, from the gleam in her eyes, Dee obviously realised that it did make it more likely that Thornton would take an active part in having her death investigated. One has, after all, a responsibility to a dead fiancée that one doesn't to a dead non-fiancée.

I was right. Once Thornton's support was gained, he made up his mind quickly and in no time at all was on the blower to the Chief Constable, who happened to be a family friend, at his ex-directory number. Then a lot of yapping to and fro and a lot of waiting. I had mentioned the name of Kenneth Graves at the Yard as being a 'sound man', with a mental apology to poor Ken who might not at all relish the thought of being posted to the wilds of Sussex while still occupied with telly and Christmas pud. If indeed, the powers that be would let him go—he might be fully occupied with the great Shoreditch Scam or the Hatton Garden Heist or the Bayswater Break-In.

'I think,' Robert Thornton announced finally, 'that we can get your friend, Detective Inspector Graves. In any case, they'll send a good man. The locals are authorising a post-mortem anyway.' He looked, for the first time, a bit white around the gills. By this time, no doubt, the 'locals' had removed Miranda. It seemed hard to believe that it was only this morning, even if in the early hours, that Dee had discovered her.

'I will, of course, be needed for questioning. Well, I'll be available.' Robert Thornton gave us a wry smile. 'It looks as if everybody at The Grange will be staying a bit longer than anticipated.'

'Yes. Or, like you, make themselves "available for questioning".' It shouldn't pose much problem, I thought. The Brewers were permanently on tap, Fitzgerald and Avery were self-employed, the Major was retired, Gabriel Field and Joyce, as research student and teacher respectively, had a long vacation, as I did myself, and Dee was not due back at the agency for a while. Of all of us, the only one who might have had some pressing professional engagement after Christmas was Miranda Travers—who was now unable to keep it.

As we made our adieux and Robert Thornton stood with us outside the front door, his face twisted in a sudden grimace of pain.

'My poor beautiful girl. She died young.'

It was now even colder and more lowering than it was before. As we drove away I asked casually, 'What was that quotation from Webster—my eyes are dazzled or something?'

'Cover her face, mine eyes dazzle, she died

young.' Dee is much better at quotations than I—
except for famous statesmen. She's an English Lit-
erature graduate and keen on drama to boot, so
she's pretty good on plays.

'That's the one. *Duchess of Malfi*, isn't it?'

'Spot on. Hardly difficult, though, Barry, it being
the one and only quote from Webster that nearly
everyone knows.'

'Including Robert Thornton?'

'I imagine so. His subconscious, perhaps, quot-
ing, or maybe he just said it off his own bat, with
no thought of a quotation. Of course,' Dee continued thoughtfully, 'Ferdinand did get Bosola to kill
the Duchess.'

'Now you've lost me.'

'Guilt at one remove. Thornton might have got
someone to do the dirty deed for him. He strikes
me a bit as one of those Browning Renaissance
types who got rid of their wives and mistresses if
they encouraged someone else. Power, allied to
good old-fashioned jealousy. "I gave commands.
Then all smiles stopped together." *My Last Duchess*. Miranda certainly smiled at other men: Gabe,
Terry, even you, darling.'

'I don't know why you say "even me",' I grumbled. 'So your theory now is that Robert Thornton
had a hired assassin. I don't really go for it. He
could do the job himself—that Mercedes would eat

up the miles, and there wouldn't be the danger of the hired one blowing the whistle.'

'Lots of other danger, though. Do we *really* suspect Robert, Barry? I suppose one has to remember he's just managed to get Scotland Yard in. Surely he'd have given us the cold shoulder if he'd had a hand in her death himself.'

'Double-bluff. Clever. Anyway, Dee, you're the one who started burbling away about Browning and Renaissance types. While you're talking about Dukes and Duchesses and such-like, what about good old Guido? Surely a more Renaissance type than Robert Thornton.'

'I don't agree. I read Guido as an impulsive charmer, both from the Santagift and from what I've heard of him. Might dot her one in the heat of the moment, but would be all flowers and remorse afterwards. Not your premeditation type at all.'

'I wonder,' I mused aloud, changing the subject, 'if Ken Graves will be on the scene by the time we get back to The Grove?'

'Surely not. They might be quick off the mark at the Yard, but I've yet to hear they issue their investigating officers with winged chariots or private planes.'

'I don't mean just yet. I thought we might stop off in Rye.'

'What for? Boxing Day—it'll be dead as a dodo.'

'Anthony Avery might be around. One wonders if he has heard the news. Also,' I pointed out, 'you haven't spent your Christmas cheque yet.'

'True.' Dee gave the truly beautiful smile which makes her look as if she is pondering spiritual truths. In fact, it is produced by a successful love-making session, a particularly good meal or the acquisition of anything she happens to fancy at that moment. Perhaps it hadn't been such a good idea after all. I had more than a suspicion that anything Dee might happen to fancy at Avery Antiques might cost more than four hundred or so pounds. Oh well—Tony Avery might have finished his stocktaking or whatever, and driven back to The Grove.

A GUSTY WIND blew down the cobbled streets of Rye. A woman battled along against it, mac flapping. Bella, who had been asleep in the back of the Mini, woke up as we parked and yelped reproachfully.

'It's OK, Bella baby,' Dee consoled her. 'You can go back to sleep.'

Avery Antiques had a wool and embroidery shop on one side, with a flat over it. On the other side was a side alleyway, so that Tony's shop was the last on that stretch of pavement. Round the side was a doorway with two bell-buttons. The sign beside one stated 'Avery Antiques'; the second merely

'Avery', from which it could be deduced that the first was a side or tradesmen's entrance to the shop and that the second was the bell for the upstairs flat. I rang both, just in case.

After a bit the door opened, and Anthony Avery stood framed in it. He was wearing dark green cords and a shaggy grey pullover and looked dusty, as if he had been opening packing cases or mending cracked plaster in the wall. He looked slightly surprised to see us, but welcomed us in. A flight of stairs led, presumably, to the upstairs quarters and a narrow corridor to the back recesses of the building.

'Come into the office,' he said, leading the way, and we followed him into a back room, which did indeed have packing cases on the floor as well as a table with sheaves of papers stuck on bill-spikes, a large ledger, pencils and pens in an onyx jar and other bits and pieces. The room also boasted a mahogany longcase clock, a couple of large display cabinets filled with porcelain and other bits and pieces, a Queen Anne slope-fronted bureau-cabinet, and a chiffonier with a beautiful set of engraved, twist-stemmed glasses behind glass doors.

'Can I offer you a glass of something?' he asked, getting out decanters and three of the precious glasses. 'Port? Sherry? Whisky? I can get water and ice from upstairs.'

'Sherry will be lovely, thank you,' said Dee in

her polite little-girl-out-to-tea voice. I agreed, and we were handed generous measures of the rich golden liquid. Anthony moved over to the desk and leaned negligently against it.

'I expect you've come to tell me about Miranda Travers' death.' We must have shown our surprise because he raised an eyebrow, smiled and added, 'Terry let me know.'

'Of course. He would have telephoned you.'

'Actually, no. The revered fuzz were swarming and poor Terence got so upset by it all he wended his way over here to tell me the dire news in person. By bus, too, as I had the BMW.'

'Oh.'

'He's gone out now. We'll be back for dinner at The Grove. I gather we may all be wanted for questioning at some stage. Not,' and he shrugged gracefully, 'that I can shed much light, I'm afraid. There seems to be some question whether she had a heart attack or something more sinister occurred—it's all rather intriguing.'

Obviously feeling that his choice of adjectives might seem a bit callous, he added, 'Of course one feels sorry about it, but it isn't as if she were someone one had known for ages. Waste of a life, and all that beauty and so on, of course. Terry is cut up—he got on well with her. A bit smitten. Which I wasn't—an attractive wench, but not my type. I've rather had my attention fixed elsewhere, over the last couple of days.' His glance flashed momentarily ceilingwards. 'An unexpected visitation, you might say.'

I nodded, with what I hoped passed for man-to-man understanding. *Cherchez* the jolly old *femme* all right. Dee tends to be right about these things.

'Actually,' I said, 'we really came to see if you were here and if we could have a look around. My wife is thinking of buying something—something small, that is,' I added hastily. Tony Avery looked amused. He probably got this approach quite a lot.

'Of course. I've got a nice little Art Deco statuette here. Four inches high, but she's quite exquisite. Preiss, carved ivory.' He reached into one of the cabinets and drew her out, holding her out on his extended palm for our admiration. The crouched nude figure, head bowed forwards, 1920s hairstyle, hands clasped gracefully in front of an outstretched leg, was indeed perfection.

'Hairline cracks,' said Tony matter-of-factly. 'Still £800, I'm afraid. These Art Deco figurines are at a premium.' He evaluated our expressions shrewdly. Dee's face had fallen. 'If you're into ivory I can do you a netsuke for £200. Look, a rather charming monkey. He is, of course, *very* tiny. Porcelain's a good investment, and I've got a Meissen cherub, not too expensive... No?' as Dee grimaced.

'I'm not into cherubs,' she explained, regarding the smug, pot-bellied little figure with disfavour.

'Perhaps you're right. They're not everyone's cup of tea. Personally I much prefer this lady,' and he drew out a shepherdess, about six inches high, if anything plain in style compared with some of the sprigged and flounced varieties, dressed in cream and maroon. 'Chelsea. A hairline crack, but almost invisible. Quite a demand for Chelsea these days. She's nice, don't you think?'

'Very,' agreed Dee. 'Er—how much is she?'

'A mere £500. To you, £470.' He gave a sudden charming smile and pointed out, 'Of course, if I knew the price range you're thinking of…'

'Anything up to £1000 for something I really like,' Dee said firmly. She had obviously decided to add some of her own money to my Christmas cheque. 'I like the Chelsea lady, but I'd like to see some more Art Deco, if you've got it.'

'But of course.' Tony Avery looked pleased. He replaced the shepherdess carefully in her cabinet and shut the door. 'As a matter of fact, I've got some new stuff in, which I've put in the front, if you'd like to follow me through. I'd recommend a Galle vase, there's a lovely one, pink on smoky grey, or there's brown on matt, and I've some Lalique, *very* sought-after now, and more figurines…' He looked doubtfully at me.

'I'll just stay here and finish my drink if I may.

I'm sure I'd just get in the way. Take your time choosing, Dee.'

Tony waved his arm in the direction of the decanters. 'Help yourself, Barry. Dee and I are going to enjoy ourselves browsing.' He led the way to the connecting door which led to the display room and they went through, leaving the door slightly ajar.

I sipped my sherry, topped it up as invited, and ambled round the office, coming to rest again before the Queen Anne desk. Idly, I tugged at the slope-front, not really expecting it to open, and surprised when it did. I had no business snooping, but I'm afraid that didn't stop me. Ever since I started this writing lark my natural snoop tendencies have quadrupled—and Dee's as bad as I am.

Inside were some small drawers, which proved to be empty except for stamps, pencil-stumps, a compass, some odd screws, and a broken fob-watch. An arched central interior revealed some old letters and postcards from different parts of the world. Voices from the front convinced me that Dee and Tony were still happily engaged examining the *objets d'art;* nevertheless I shoved the correspondence back guiltily. As I did so my clumsy fingers brushed over a protuberance in the wood, and a panel slid back, startling me. Of course these old bureaux tend to have secret cavities and I had obviously inadvertently just discovered one. Moreover, it was not empty.

A careful look at the door reassured me that it was only ajar about two or three inches, and, moreover, the desk and I were out of the immediate eyeline, if I stood to the side of the desk instead of in front. Which I did, my prying busybody fingers swiftly unwrapping the tissue paper and revealing what was beneath.

It was a bronze statuette, about 28 centimetres high, including the circular plinth. It depicted a nude young man, in a negligent posture, one leg slightly in front of the other. Every detail was breathtakingly perfect, from the curls on the head and the classical features to the winged sandals on the feet and the loose curl of the fingers. No prizes for guessing it was Mercury, messenger of the Gods—what might be more difficult to determine was what century it was and its value. I guessed a nineteenth century copy, in miniature, of a much earlier work, the bronze newly cleaned. Value was difficult to assess—Dee might be better at that than I was. In any case, it was, I would guess, beyond our means, even if it had been on public display.

I carefully wrapped the tissue paper round it and replaced it in the drawer, which I pushed in. There was a faint 'click' and it was hidden once more. I shut the desk, and took up my stance in front of it, glass in one hand, the other elbow leaning along the top of the desk, just the way Tony Avery had been leaning, before he moved over to the cabinet to draw out some of the items to show us. Come to think of it, the way he had been standing might very well have shown a desire to protect the contents of the desk, until he lost himself in the desire to make a sale. Perhaps there was another secret cavity in it, with some other beautiful thing inside. I imagined Avery Antiques was comprehensively insured; certainly the sum total of the furniture and other items would come to a very hefty sum indeed. But, of course, that applied to many antique shops, even those less lavishly stocked.

Dee had a flush on her face and a satisfied air, as of one who had bargained long and hard and worn down the opposition. Tony Avery looked resigned. He gave me a wry smile.

'Better get the lady to write out the cheque immediately, before I change my mind. She certainly appreciates beauty—and value.'

'What did you get, Dee?' I demanded anxiously as she signed her name with a flourish on the cheque, tore it out and handed it to Avery with her Barclaycard.

'The jade horse.'

I groaned.

'*Significantly* reduced.' Anthony Avery was obviously regretting the sale. Dee grabbed my arm and held her hand out to him.

'Thank you so much for your time and patience, Tony. It was simply fascinating listening to you—

and needless to say I shall *treasure* my horse. You
don't need a lift back to The Grove, do you? No,
of course, you're waiting for Terry and you'll come
in the BMW.' She burbled on as we edged towards
the door.

I guess I may have looked pretty sheepish, too,
in view of my late activities inside the Queen Anne
bureau. In any case, we both heaved a sigh of relief
when we had been shown out. Dee was carefully
clutching a brown parcel which looked as if it had
a lot of wadding underneath. The horse.

'I'll drive,' Dee offered cheerfully. 'You look after Pegasus and keep an eye on Bella. She might
want to spend a penny *en route.*'

'Talking of pennies,' I began, as Dee reversed,
drew out and drove off with a flourish, with a parting wave to the door of Avery Antiques. 'How
much?'

'Only nine hundred.' She had the grace to look
a teeny bit abashed.

'*Only!* Words fail me.'

'Worth more and likely to climb skywards in the
next few weeks. Regard it as an investment, Barry.
We'll just have to eat a lot of cabbage and mince
next month, that's all.'

I groaned again. I hate cabbage. And I'm not
wild about mince either. But I knew I looked as
resigned as Tony Avery had. And the horse—Peg-

asus, as Dee had aptly named it—*would* look impressive in the living-room at Elmtree Avenue.

'I hope you weren't too bored waiting for me back in the office, darling. You should have come with us. Tony is really very interesting when he gets going. He seems immensely knowledgeable and has a passion for antiques.'

'Oh, I wasn't bored,' I said truthfully. I decided to keep my little snoop-around to myself. For the present, anyway.

NINE

Detective Inspector Graves at The Grove

DETECTIVE INSPECTOR Kenneth Graves had a short four-day break at Christmas. He could have taken longer, but opted for a long summer break this year. He had spent Christmas with Elizabeth Fane—charming, graceful Elizabeth, whom he had met through Dee Vaughan—the best thing to emerge from the imbroglio at Wentworth Hall, last year. They were on the way to becoming a couple, he thought. Certainly, they had spent part of Boxing Day poring over travel brochures, deciding where they would spend the summer holiday—together. Until the phone rang. The Big White Chief with orders to proceed to a place called East Peasmarsh in Sussex. To a hotel called The Grove. The fiancée of an industrialist had died in what appeared to be suspicious circumstances, and he was demanding Yard action. Well, requesting it. His family were influential in Sussex, golf with the Chief Constable and so on, and the girl who had died had been a well-known international model. Moreover, there was nothing pressing in London which Ken could not delegate, and, to cap it all, he had been mentioned by name by this Thornton fellow—of whom he had heard, but certainly not imagined that the reverse would hold good. It was, apparently, something to do with the ubiquitous Vaughans, who were staying at The Grove themselves. Ken didn't know whether to laugh or be annoyed.

'At any rate they'll brief you on what's been going on, and on all the guests,' Elizabeth consoled him. 'Think of it as a dynamic partnership, Ken! If I know Dee she'll be half-way to sorting it out already. Trust her and Barry to be in on the action! I wish I were going with you.'

'So do I.' He kissed her appreciatively. 'Did I ever tell you you're rather beautiful?'

'Yes. Only, the last time, it was "very", not "rather". Am I going off, or something?'

'Quite the reverse. Sorry to dash off like this, Elizabeth. I'm afraid it's not an infrequent occurrence, in the life of a copper.' At the back of his mind was the thought that it was as well she was getting used to it. If things moved on towards marriage, as seemed possible, then she'd be a copper's wife, with all the attendant inconveniences.

'Think nothing of it.' She patted his hand. 'But ring me when you can, won't you?'

He promised.

'THERE'S NO PEACE for the wicked,' Ken sighed, much, much later, having been on the go since parting from Elizabeth. He had arrived at The Grove by car, with Sergeant Ian Anderson (likewise snatched from the home comforts of Christmas pud and telly) in attendance. There he had met Inspector Townsend of the local force, and been filled in. Photographing of the corpse of Miranda Travers from various angles had taken place before it was removed, and the table which the doctor thought she had struck her head against had been examined by forensic boys, who had yet to put in their report.

The body of Miranda Travers having been removed for the post-mortem, a chalk outline was left on the carpet, marking the place where it had lain. Looking up at the ornate brass chandelier, with the large piece of mistletoe dangling from it, and then down at the stark chalked outline which represented the pathetic corpse of the girl who had been lying beneath, Ken shivered. It was the unintentionally gruesome touches that got to you. There seemed something almost obscene about that mistletoe. He caught young Ian Anderson looking at him with an expression of understanding, and grimaced.

'Seems a bit horrible, Ian, somehow. I mean, Christmas—carols and fun and games and goodwill to all—and now this.'

'Yes, sir. Pretty lass, too.'

'Indeed.' Not, Ken reflected, that it made much difference if a woman was pretty or not, or young or not. Death was still a tragedy; it just seemed more so. And of course, Christmas might be the season of goodwill, but it was also a time for break-ins, burglaries, family quarrels and sometimes violence provoked by the strain of over-eating, pretended jollity and the unremitting company of people who suddenly found so much more to dislike in each other than when they were apart for the rest of the year. Usually verbal violence, but not always.

'Well, Ian, time to call a halt, I think.'

Anderson's face brightened. 'Yes, *sir*,' he agreed with enthusiasm.

Two small, unoccupied single rooms on the ground floor had been put at their disposal, and they retired there with tray suppers provided by Betty Brewer after the drawing-room had been sealed off. Muted clattering and conversation came from the dining-room, but Ken did not judge it politic for them to join the guests, not on the first evening, anyway. In fact, it would probably be better if he and Ian drove along the road to that inn they had passed, for meals. Apart from breakfast, that is. He was damned if he was going to miss out on breakfast—the guests would just have to put up with the presence of a couple of flatties.

The next day promised to be packed with action, too—the fingerprint boys were arriving, and at least some preliminary interviewing of guests could take place. They might have to wait some time for the findings of the post-mortem, but there were Townsend and his cronies to liaise with—and, of course, at some stage the Vaughans would be poking their eager noses in.

'Sufficient unto the day is the evil thereof,' he wisely informed Ian Anderson, who was stifling a huge yawn.

'Yes, sir.' Anderson could wax lyrical on occasion, but he was a Scot, and normally a man of few words. 'Yes, sir' were the most frequently uttered.

THE AFTERMATH of Christmas is usually one of hangovers, indigestion, sluggishness, and when one recovers from these, pleasant idleness sets in. Not, however, when one is a suspect in a murder case.

The discovery of Miranda's dead body, the subsequent visits by Dr Fry and Inspector Townsend, the descent of the men from the Yard and the sealing-off of the drawing-room were gradual shocks to the system slowly absorbed by the inhabitants of The Grove. The gravity of the situation was dawning on them when they noted the appearance of two strangers at the breakfast table, and by the time they had been rounded up for fingerprinting there could be no doubt about the fact that Miranda Travers was not considered to have died a natural death.

Unpleasant though it was, the inhabitants of The Grove were suspects. They could react with fear, hostility, righteous indignation or whatever. There might have been some bluster, but they submitted. After all, as Gabriel remarked to Joyce, no-one wants to appear to have anything to hide, and there's no point in drawing attention to oneself.

Townsend's search of Miranda's room had turned up a container of digitalis tablets in the bathroom, about three-quarters empty. A variety of fingerprints were found all over the various surfaces in the drawing-room—on the other hand, the handle of the French window revealed only the deceased's.

'Looks as if she opened the window to someone, doesn't it, sir?' volunteered Ian Anderson, his face flushed now that the excitement of the chase had begun and he was part of it.

'Of course, Miranda could have been the last to touch the French window from inside the night before—before they all went off after the charades or what-have-you.' Ken had received a version of the evening's happenings by this time, both from the Brewers and from Major Gardner, so far the most friendly of the Grove guests—with the exception of the Vaughans, with whom he had not yet chewed the fat. Ian's face fell, but brightened again as Ken added, 'But it certainly looks as if she not only touched the handle but grasped it pretty firmly since then, and as you point out, Ian, the obvious deduction is that she was opening it for somebody.'

'Which in turn presupposes a pre-arranged assignation.'

'Precisely. And Dee Vaughan apparently found the French window not ajar, but slightly off the latch. Which means that the person she let in *could* have knocked her out and slipped out again, covering his hand with either the glove he was wearing or a handkerchief, and drawing the window to behind him. He would not, of course, have been able to latch it, since that could be done only from the inside.'

'That rules out her striking her head against the table, though, sir.'

'Not necessarily.' Graves did not expand, but added quickly, 'I think we'll see the Brewers again, Ian.'

The two Brewers were still upset and bewildered. They described Miranda as an attractive girl who obviously liked the limelight and grabbed as much attention as she could.

'Bit of a troublemaker, if you ask me,' Robin said thoughtfully. 'I mean, she'd flirt with this one and that one, and it wouldn't mean much to her. But I'd have said she loved life. I certainly can't imagine her doing away with herself.' Robin Brewer knew about the discovery of the nearly-empty container of digitalis in Miranda's room.

'We don't know that she did,' Ken pointed out gently.

Betty revealed that Miranda had asked for a flask of cocoa before she retired on Christmas night. She didn't know if all the cocoa had been drunk, but certainly the flask and plastic cup-top had been washed out. Graves sighed.

'It'll have to be checked for fingerprints.' However, he wasn't very hopeful of finding any beside Betty's and Miranda's.

Further questioning elicited the story of the alarm going off in the middle of the night, and the fact that Miranda had not emerged from her room.

'So she could have had someone in there with her?'

Betty admitted that it was possible. She confirmed that she had checked the French window in the drawing-room herself after the guests had drifted off for the night, and had been sure it was fastened securely. If Miranda's prints were firmly superimposed, this lent additional weight to the theory that Miranda had gone down and opened the French window at some later stage, either before the alarm had gone off, or considerably after. So— had she made one visit to the drawing-room or two? She could have let in someone, kept him in her room and let him out later, opening the French window to do so.

'Said person having been completely innocent, Ian—at any rate of any attack on Miranda. So, did she get hit on the head by someone completely different, from inside the hotel in all probability (I mean, the theory of an intruder on top of the assignation bod seems a lot to swallow)? Or are we back to square one with Miranda going into her heart attack before receiving the contusions on the head, and merely hitting her head on the table as she went down?'

'I'm blest if I know, sir.'

'I'm blest if I know either. But forensic might shed some light, in due course. Not to mention the results of the post-mortem. The moment the digitalis entered the case, Ian, it became, theoretically at least, a lot more complicated than the heart-attack-brought-on-by-fright idea. Not that that would be very feasible in a girl of her age, anyway, even with a weak heart. *Even* consequent on an attack. Even Mr Brewer latched onto the notion of a suicidal overdose of digitalis, though saying it wasn't likely.'

'And from there it's just a short step to an overdose given by someone else, you mean, sir?'

'Exactly. I wonder if it was Miranda who washed that cocoa flask clean—or someone who was in there with her?'

'You mean she might have been supping up cocoa laced with digitalis with her murderer, sir, while the others were flapping round trying to get the alarm turned off?'

Ken looked at his sergeant approvingly. 'Well—it's certainly a possibility, wouldn't you say?'

'Yes, sir.'

'Just like old times,' Dee remarked nostalgically.

She and Barry were in the living-room with Ken and his sergeant, the latter hovering unobtrusively in the background with his notebook on his knee. They were drinking tea from a very nice Crown Derby set and consuming ham and cucumber sandwiches and sponge fingers, provided by the ever-thoughtful Brewers.

'If by that,' observed Ken tartly, 'you mean that where you two are there is trouble, then I agree with you. Red for danger.' He gazed at Dee's abundance of curling chestnut locks with a jaundiced eye. Dee curled up with her feet beneath her on the big chair and gave him a winning and forgiving beam.

'Now, now, Ken, we don't *cause* the trouble, you know. I mean, can we help it if people happen to get killed in places we stay?' Since the question was obviously rhetorical she didn't pause for an answer, but plunged on. 'You're looking handsomer than ever—positively the Yard's answer to Paul Newman, do you know that?'

'And that's another thing,' Ken went on, loftily ignoring her blandishments. 'If it hadn't been for you two and your precious pal Mr Robert Thornton, I would have been spending the Christmas break—

the very hard-earned Christmas break, I may say—
with my nearest and dearest, instead of...'

'Oh, yes,' Dee interposed sweetly, 'and how *is*
Elizabeth?'

'Her delightful self, and even more so. She was
very good about my rushing off at a moment's notice.'

'There you are then. Aren't you glad I introduced
you?'

An unwilling smile touched Ken's lips. 'Very.
But to return to...'

'And another thing. Robert Thornton isn't a pal
of ours. We only met him yesterday. And I don't
think we like him much, do we, darling? But we
did feel that Miranda's death was distinctly fishy,
and he had the influence to demand a real, gen-u-
ine honest-to-God Scotland Yard detective be
posted to the spot. And since you're the best there
is...'

'Since you're the only one we know,' chipped in
Barry, 'we naturally mentioned your name.'

'So here I am,' Ken said sardonically.

'So here you are,' Barry agreed placidly. 'So
don't you want our eyewitnesses' on-the-spot account?'

Ian Anderson's eyes had been popping out during this exchange. Ken turned and smiled reassuringly at him.

'It's all right, Ian—Laurel and Hardy here aren't

just a comic turn. They may actually be able to help, believe it or not.'

'So what,' Barry enquired agreeably, 'do you want us to start with? Our ideas about the people here, or how we first saw Miranda Travers in Florence, or significant incidents like the Woolly Scarf Threat?'

'Or the Case of the Missing Santagram. Or the Alarm that Went Off in the Night.' It was Dee's turn. Ken held up his hand.

'Hold on, hold on. This sounds fascinating. But since the only one that rings a bell—not to make too awful a pun—is the Alarm that Went Off in the Night, I think you'd better start there. And since I hardly think you two can seriously be considered as suspects, just so that you don't accuse me of holding out on you, I'd better tell you now that there is some suspicion that Miranda Travers died as a result of a hefty dose of digitalis, the medication she had for her heart, administered by some person unknown. It's a possibility that she had someone in her room with her during the Alarm Incident. Which would be a very good reason for her not to come out to see what was going on, as you did.'

'A lover, you mean?' Barry demanded.

'Or, at any rate, someone she'd let into her room, possibly to discuss something. This person could have been let in by Miranda downstairs, through the French windows here.' The Vaughans' two heads automatically swivelled round towards the window.

'That's only a hypothesis, of course,' Ken added. 'It seems possible she let someone in at some stage. It could have been the person who was in her room, or if the person who was in her room came from inside the hotel, then it could have been someone different, later. That person might have hit her on the head, but was unlikely to have administered the fatal dose, since digitalis takes some time to be absorbed into the system. In fact, whoever it was probably gave her more than the one dosage.'

'But if it was the person in her room, the people who came out to see what was going on might be eliminated, you mean?'

'Not necessarily. We're only *assuming* there was someone in her room, for the present. But it's a starting point. Put it this way. If there *was* anyone in her room, he or she was up to *something*, even if it was only a heart-to-heart chat, and *might* have been putting digitalis tablets in her cocoa or whatever. All right,' Ken added crossly, seeing their sceptical expressions. 'I know it's far-fetched. But like I said—'

'One has to start somewhere!' Dee and Barry chorused.

There was a pause for refreshments, and then Barry began to tell Ken what had happened.

'Major Gardner came out of number nine and Terry Fitzgerald out of number eleven, about the same time as Dee and I emerged. Dee stayed at the door for a bit and then went back to bed while I went off with the Major to get the Brewers. Robin came back with me, but I saw Betty as well. Nobody else emerged, but the sound would have been muffled to anyone not on our floor, so Miranda was the only other one who would have been expected to come out.'

Ken nodded. 'And that leaves?'

'Joyce Bradley and Gabriel Field. They're in rooms One and Two on the ground floor. Morgan Grant had been staying in the hotel the night before—Christmas Eve—but he went back to his B&B in Rye during Christmas Day. Anthony Avery wasn't in his room, obviously, or he'd have turned off the alarm—anyway, I went in with Robin Brewer and it was empty. Anthony has an antiques shop in Rye and apparently he had some urgent stocktaking or something to do there and decided to spend the night in his flat above the shop. He probably forgot all about the digital alarm; anyway he'd obviously set it for entirely the wrong time in the first place.'

'Of course,' added Barry, 'it would have been a wonderful way to establish an alibi, wouldn't it? I mean, to make sure everyone knew he wasn't in the hotel that night. So, if he *were* the one Miranda let in…but he didn't like her much, nor she him, I'm pretty sure. Whereas Morgan Grant, who was sweet on her since the year dot, would have been much more likely to get into her bed, or at any rate into her room. He might have phoned up from his B&B, all miserable and regretting leaving the hotel, and she might have said "Come on up and see me sometime", or words to that effect. The fact that she was engaged to Robert Thornton and pursued by an Italian called Guido di Montefalcone, whom she'd been very actively encouraging, wouldn't necessarily stop her taking on Morgan as a lover, if only as a consolation prize. She'd probably have seen it as the big, magnanimous gesture of her life.'

'Barry, darling,' Dee interposed. 'I really do think you ought to stop and fill Ken in on who and what all these people are. Methodically, I mean. He must be getting terribly confused, and, after all, we do know quite a bit about them.'

'Perhaps you'd like to volunteer for the task, Dee,' the Detective-Inspector suggested, leaning back in his chair. 'Woman's viewpoint and so on. And my invaluable Sergeant Anderson will take notes.'

'Right.' Dee took a deep breath. 'Where shall I start—or rather, with whom?'

'Miranda Travers?'

'OK. I think I'd better begin at the beginning, which was the Uffizi Gallery in Florence. Well…'

Ken Graves listened, lounging back in a deceptively languid manner, but fully alert. Now that he'd got stuck with this wretched case, he needed to know as much as possible about these people…

TEN

The Case Continues

Detective Inspector Graves

'AND SO,' finished Barry, 'someone was trying to frighten Miranda in a particularly nasty way. And succeeded. But it could be a red herring. Some people like to play sadistic games—and come to think of it, Murder in the Dark is a pretty scary game itself. There might not even be any malice specifically directed against Miranda as a person. I mean, she might just have been the first person the joker came across in the dark.'

'I'm inclined to agree,' Ken said. He was still reclining at ease, but Dee and Barry could be certain that his sharp mind had taken in every scrap of information and every shade of opinion Dee had given him about Miranda and the other guests at The Grove. When Dee had shown signs of flagging Barry had taken over, his commentary culminating in the Woolly Scarf Threat.

'Anyway,' Ken went on, 'I might be inclined to treat it as being of more relevance if Miranda had been strangled—especially with a scarf. But she wasn't. So it's more likely to have been a piece of ill-natured fooling which the person may have regretted afterwards, when Miranda really did die. Still—we can't entirely rule out the fact that if our assumptions about the digitalis are correct, this killing was premeditated to some extent, not just a quick knife-in-the-ribs sort of affair. The killer *might* have wanted to make Miranda sweat, fearing her life was in danger, but would have known that his fooling-around with the scarf would have been treated by everybody as just an extension of the Murder in the Dark game, even if he was found out. There might have been a few tut-tuts, and that's all.'

Dee uttered a long and elaborate sigh. 'Everything seems to be "might have been" and "if" in this case,' she complained crossly. 'It's altogether too iffy for my liking.'

Ken grinned and gave her the kind of glance Paul Newman as Butch Cassidy might have given the Sundance Kid when the latter was throwing a tantrum. 'Sorry madam, but it's just the start of things yet, you know. We've only just got here. However, with you and Barry helping out, everything ought to be wrapped up before the New Year.'

'Well, we haven't much in the way of theories, yet,' Dee confessed. 'I expect we'll just have to await further developments.'

There was a hesitant, but prolonged knock at the door.

'Come in,' Ken called. The tall, spare figure of Major Gardner advanced into the room. Without seeming even to notice Barry and Dee, he fixed a worried gaze on Ken.

'I'm sorry to disturb you, Detective Inspector Graves,' he began, 'but I'm a bit concerned about something. It's my pills, you see—my heart pills. I left them in the bathroom on my corridor on Christmas Day, and they disappeared. I thought I must have left them somewhere else, but I searched everywhere and the more I think about it, the more certain I am that I left them there. I asked Mrs. Brewer, but she said quite definitely that she hadn't taken them or seen them at all, and apart from making the beds, nobody's been seeing to the rooms since Christmas Day, what with, well, what with—everything—' His voice trailed tactfully off. 'And—well—they could be dangerous to someone else, you see.' His long, kindly face, which always reminded Dee of the pictures of medieval saints, looked more worried than ever.

'But, Major,' Dee broke in impulsively, 'isn't it very bad for you, not having your pills? Surely you're meant to take them every day—and if this is the third day without them...'

'Oh, that's all right, Mrs Vaughan.' Major Gardner turned towards her and smiled gratefully. 'But how kind of you to be concerned. I have spares, you see, in a little box, and I always carry it round with me. My daughter gave it to me—look.' He reached into his trousers pocket and pulled out an enamelled box in blue and gold. 'Pretty little thing, isn't it? Antique, too, I believe. However, it doesn't hold many of the things, and unfortunately I'm down to my last three. Of course, I can get the prescription made up in Rye, but it's inconvenient and I might have to wait. So that's another reason I'm worried.'

'May I see?' Ken stretched out his hand, and, rather surprised, the Major put the box on his open palm.

'Thank you.' He pushed the spring and the lid flew open. Ken drew in his breath sharply. Inside were three orange capsules.

'But these aren't pills—they're capsules!'

The Major now looked totally uncomprehending. 'Well, yes—pills, capsules, much the same thing, surely?'

There was another knock on the door, quite a loud, imperative one, and Betty Brewer's voice was heard calling, ''Scuse me, Inspector, phone for you. Can you take it at the desk, it's important.'

Ken strode out. Sergeant Anderson wriggled and cleared his throat. The Major contemplated his shoes gloomily. Dee opened her mouth as if to ask a question, thought better of it, and shut it again.

Barry folded his arms and sat back in a detached manner. They all waited.

It was some minutes later when Ken returned. He had lost his previous frustrated air, Dee thought.

'Major Gardner may I ask you to describe the container your capsules were in.'

The Major considered. 'Well, just one of those ordinary round plastic things they give you at the chemist's. Brownish, with a white lid. Quite a big one. About three inches, I suppose.' He demonstrated with his thumb and index finger.

'Hardly to be confused with one this size, I imagine.' The Detective Inspector produced another container, about the same height but about one-third of the width.

'Good Heavens, no,' Gardner agreed emphatically.

'And did your container have the label on the front giving the details of the medication and dosage—or had it come off?'

'It had the label, which was perfectly readable.'

'One more question, Major. Are your capsules a form of digitalin?'

'Yes, they are. Digitoxin. Look, what...'

'I know. What on earth is all this about? Well, Major the phone call I just had was to confirm the results of the post-mortem on Miranda Travers. She was suffering from a congestive heart condition and, according to her own doctor, her last prescription for digitalis medication was made up some time ago. That means that if she was taking her three tablets a day regularly, there would only have been a few left in the container—perhaps more than we found, but not many more. It looks as if she took her own pills earlier, and a further dosage of even a few capsules, say three or four, would have done the trick: Digitoxin on top of her own digitalis pills, producing overdose and cardiac arrest. I imagine the contents of the capsules were removed (this would be a simple matter) and dissolved in liquid, which was then given to Miranda. No wonder you can't find your capsules, Major. Though, come to think of it, what surprises me is that the container with the remaining capsules hasn't reappeared. If only three or four were taken out you would hardly miss them if the container was even half-full. Was it?'

The Major nodded, looking white and shaken.

'More than half-full—about three-quarters. My God, I'll never forgive myself for leaving them there! But are you sure, Graves?'

Ken shrugged. 'Pretty sure. A few pills from her own lot, though they would have paved the way for heart failure, would have needed a strong additional dose to finish things off. We have Miranda's own pills—what's left of them—and if she had taken the remaining pills it might just have produced the same effect, on top of what she'd had already. But it was so much surer with your capsules... May I take one from your pill-box, as a sample? Thank you. I'm afraid you're going to have to try to replace them by prescription at the chemist's now. We can hardly hope that they'll suddenly reappear, complete with incriminating fingerprints.'

The Major did not look amused. He was regaining his colour, but after handing Ken the capsule, had retreated to a chair where he sat down heavily and muttered to himself, 'Terrible...incredible... doesn't bear thinking about...'

'Cheer up, Major. You can't hold yourself responsible—it's hardly criminal negligence to leave one's medication in the bathroom one shares with other guests. But you should have made more of a fuss about it before.'

'I realise that.' The Major nodded humbly. 'I suppose...I don't suppose there's any possibility the girl took the dose herself?'

'Suicide being marginally better than murder, you mean? Afraid not. We've been waiting for this confirmation of post-mortem findings. I suspected digitalis poisoning, but didn't want to proceed with questioning until it was made certain. What was your own impression of the young lady, by the way, Major? And her relations with her fellow-guests here. Forget about *de mortuis* and all that, sir. We want to arrive at the truth and we won't do that by pussyfooting around.'

Thus addressed, the Major gathered himself together and straightened his shoulders.

'A flibbertigibbet. No, that's too innocent. Pretty
as a picture and charming when she chose to be,
but calculating, was my impression. Flirted with
Terence Fitzgerald, though it's my opinion he's a
lady's man and it's routine to him, so it wouldn't
harm him. Kept that artist fellow, Grant, dancing
to her tune and was doing a line with young Gabriel
Field at the same time. Now that *was* unnecessary,
and malicious, too. It not only put Grant's nose out
of joint, it upset young Field's—er—lady-friend.'

'I see. Upset her or Grant enough to tempt them
to do away with her, perhaps.'

The Major shot him a penetrating glance and
merely said, with some contempt, 'Preposterous.'

'Perhaps. Perhaps not. There are stranger things
in heaven and earth, than…'

'Oh, for Heaven's sake, Graves, don't quote Hor-
atio at me!' the Major exclaimed tartly. 'We are a
relatively civilised people, after all. People don't
kill just because of a little flirtation, even if it makes
them angry.'

'In Grant's case, it may have been a culmination
of indiscretions and involvements over the last couple of years. The proverbial last straw. Someone
put a scarf round her neck during the Charades
game and said, ''You're going to die, Miranda''.
Even if neither Grant nor Miss Bradley, Field's

"lady-friend" as you delicately put it, would actually commit murder, don't you think either of them had enough provocation to play a trick on her and frighten her—that probably being all that was intended?'

This time the Major wasn't so sure. He protested Joyce Bradley's patent innocence, but in a slightly less sure tone of voice, and admitted that, for all he knew, it might be the kind of thing Grant could get up to.

'He's a bit of a weird specimen, anyway, though that's only my personal opinion, you understand.'

Barry's voice broke in, startling them.

'And you, yourself, Major Gardner, said to me that something bad would happen to Miranda Travers one of these days, and that she needed a lesson. Might you not have twisted a scarf round her neck and whispered a scary message to her, just to frighten her and "give her a lesson"? Extreme measures, perhaps, but might it not have made her reflect on the fact she was playing with fire and making people hostile—even making them hate her?'

Major Gardner gasped indignantly. 'Of course not! I'd never do a thing like that. I might have taken her aside and warned her she was hurting people and making them antagonistic, but...'

'But she wouldn't have taken the slightest bit of notice, would she? She'd either have laughed at you, or been sweetly patronising and told you she could look after herself, and not to be such a Victorian old dear. A better strategy was needed, Major, and I've no doubt that whoever thought it up did have a certain amount of success. Miranda spoke to me just after the incident and there's no doubt that she was badly shaken.'

'Well, I didn't do it, strategy or no strategy. I'm fond of Joyce Bradley and I didn't like seeing her hurt, but not fond or foolish enough to indulge in bizarre theatrical gestures like that,' the Major returned with spirit, before turning appealingly to Ken.

'Detective-Inspector, do they have to be here?' Dee and Barry were favoured with a frosty glare.

'Er—quite right, Major. Apologies. But I've finished with you for the moment, anyway. I may require a statement later about your whereabouts in the early hours of the morning of the 26th.'

'Well, *that's* simple enough. I was in bed. Asleep. Except when that blasted alarm went off, of course. Took me about a quarter of an hour to get back to sleep afterwards. But of course you'll have heard about the alarm already, from Mr Vaughan here.' And the Major strode out of the room, shooting the Vaughans another cold glance before he left.

'Oh dear, Barry, you weren't exactly the soul of tact,' Dee murmured ruefully.

'No, I suppose not.' Barry's voice was a mite faraway. 'By the way, Ken, I should add to my comment that the Woolly Scarf Threat had achieved a certain amount of success, the fact that, according to Robert Thornton, she accepted his proposal of marriage on the phone on Christmas Day. The Woolly Scarf incident may well have been the turning point. She may have felt she needed the protection of marriage at this point; measured it against the delights of endless conquests and found those delights wanting—or too dangerous. The person in her bedroom in the wee small hours may have been the final fling.'

'Final in every sense,' Dee reminded soberly.

'True.'

'And of course there's no proof that the person in the bedroom administered the fatal dose. In fact, there's no proof that there *was* a person in the bedroom at all. True, it seems the most likely explanation why Miranda didn't come beetling out at a hundred miles per hour like the rest of us when she heard that alarm. But on the other hand, she might have been in a deep sleep. Or, knowing Miranda, just waiting for someone else to get things sorted out.'

'Hmmm. If I can interrupt you two...'

'Oh, interrupt away,' Barry said cheerfully. 'You are in charge of the case, after all.'

'Kind of you to mention it. I was about to say

that I think it might be a good idea if you absented yourself from this room. People being questioned aren't going to take kindly to your presence—let alone your popping eyes and flapping ears and the odd comment thrown in here and there.'

'We couldn't hide under the table?'

'Certainly not. Oh, and Ian…'

'Yes, sir?' The young sergeant leapt to attention.

'Find something to cover up the chalk outline on the carpet, will you, there's a good man. People are likely to find it unnerving.'

'Yes, sir.'

Barry and Dee got up with dignity.

'You will let us know if anything interesting happens? Any vital new information?' Dee enquired anxiously.

'Of course.' Ken Graves had a twinkle in his eye. 'In fact, I had one new item via the phone just then, apart from the post-mortem results. Apparently traces of Miranda's blood and hair were found on the corner edge of the side table.'

'So the doctor was right,' Barry reflected thoughtfully. 'She *did* strike her head on it going down.'

'So it would appear. Frankly,' Ken said soberly, 'I'm not one hundred percent in favour of that solution. The angle of the body in relation to the table, for one thing. Decidedly awkward. Not impossible, but awkward.'

'So you think someone bashed her with the table—possibly to make it look like an accident, all fitting in with the natural heart attack theory?'

'Could be. According to the doctor's report, as far as can be determined death took place sometime between three and five in the morning. The first signs of rigor don't set in for a long time, anyway, but given that she was cold when you touched her, Dee, or so I understand, she had been dead for a while when you got there. Of course the draught from the open French window would have chilled the process more quickly, so to speak, but on the other hand there was the central heating. Anyway, an attempt was made to make the death look like a natural heart attack, with Miranda overdosing with her own pills maybe while drunk and keeling over in here and snuffing it, banging her head en route. All set up quite nicely, and if the person was resident in the hotel, the open French window could be an attempt to suggest an intruder, or a visit by someone known to Miranda from outside, who either left before she hit the floor, or who panicked and got out.

'The discovery of the Major's capsules having disappeared makes murder and malice aforethought more positive. Bad luck for the murderer. But now our task is that much easier, because we know that the capsules must have been given to Miranda prior to death. Easier, did I say! Everyone will of course, like the Major, say they were in bed and asleep; impossible either to prove or disprove.'

'Morgan Grant or Anthony Avery might have an alibi. Or—someone might have seen one of them making for The Grove, up to no good,' Dee suggested.

'Well—all in due course. And now, I really am going to boot you two out.'

'All right, all right, we're going. Come on, Dee.'

'Don't you think it's a bit—well—gruesome, seeing them in here, Ken? Surely the Brewers would let you have another room?'

'I daresay they would. But people who are upset by the proximity to where a dead body was a short while ago are more likely to let things slip.'

'You horrid inquisitor!'

'Well—it goes with the job, Dee. Our aim is to reveal the truth, you know. Wouldn't you say the end justifies the means?'

A CONSIDERABLE time later, a hungry and tired Detective Inspector and his Sergeant decided to close up shop and repair up the road for a ploughman's and something strong to go with it.

'Got your notes all sorted, lad?'

'Yes, sir.'

'Good fellow. Well, as inconclusive as I'd thought, at this stage, except we did get some feedback with Avery and Miss Bradley—Ms Bradley, I should say.'

Gabriel hadn't been much help. He said he'd liked Miranda.

'She was kind of trying to be a free spirit, know what I mean, and grabbing at the goodies as well. I felt a bit sorry for her. She hadn't learned yet you've got to opt for one lifestyle or another.' He admitted his relationship with Miranda had been getting warmer, and to kissing her under the mistletoe.

'Though, frankly, Inspector, I don't want to sound what in the past they used to call a "cad", but it was her grabbing me, rather than the other way round. I didn't really enjoy it, because I knew Joyce would be upset.'

Questioned further he was forthright, in a vague sort of way.

'Look, Joyce and I aren't lovers, but I wouldn't mind. It just hasn't happened, that's all. I'd marry her, only I think someone else would be better for her. I'm not bothered about having no money—she doesn't mind, and I might have sometime, win the Pools or something. But she really needs someone older. Someone a bit like the Major, only younger than him, of course, and not so stuffy. A sort of middle-aged, middle-of-the-road person who's a gentleman, but trendy without being flash, if you know what I mean.'

No, he'd no motive to wish Miranda dead. Yes, he'd been to her room once, while she picked up a handkerchief or something. It had been pretty untidy, lots of scent and stuff on the dressing-table and an old toy panda. Yes, she had told him she had a heart condition, but he wasn't sure if she was play-acting or not. It's the kind of thing she might have said to get sympathy or to make herself more 'interesting'. Yes, he might have mentioned it to someone, he couldn't remember. Hardly Joyce; Miranda was a forbidden topic between them. No, he hadn't been in her bathroom or seen any pills, and no, he hadn't seen any pills in the bathroom on the floor above. He slept very soundly and hadn't heard an alarm or anything on Christmas night, though he *had* been woken up early the next morning by that little dog of Dee Vaughan's barking. Naturally he was shocked by Miranda's death, but after all he hadn't known her very well, and when the hell could they get out of this place, please?

Terry Fitzgerald's account was even more inconclusive. He'd been woken by the digital alarm at 1.15 a.m. and when it was stopped he'd gone back to bed and got to sleep. It hadn't been easy; he'd started to read a historical novel and that sent him off after about half an hour. He hadn't heard anything further along the corridor and hadn't gone out of his room again till the next morning at about

8.30, for breakfast, which was when he'd heard about Miranda. Horrible thing. Ravishing kid—yes, they'd been flirting, but that was as far as it had gone.

He could confirm that Anthony had a lot to do at the shop and he had to do the books among other things; also there had been a delivery he had to check, so, although Christmas night seemed a weird time to rush off to the office, it was understandable in a way, especially since old Anthony got easily bored, and he didn't exactly find the company riveting at The Grove. Also there was a lady involved, but they'd find that out for themselves from Anthony.

He hadn't known of Miranda's heart condition and didn't know of any pills of any kind, hadn't seen any; thank goodness *he* was healthy and didn't need anything like that. Couldn't think who would want Miranda dead, seemed a harmless kid, was sure they'd find it was natural causes, well, not *murder* anyway. No, he hadn't ever been in Miranda's room, and, repeat, he was not having an affair with her.

Joyce Bradley had been on the defensive. Her eyes had immediately strayed to the sheet-covered place on the carpet where Sergeant Anderson had covered the chalked outline of the corpse. She shuddered and turned, if possible, a little paler. Invited to sit down, she had done so carefully, ankles primly crossed, hands loosely joined in her lap, but the fingers had started twisting nervously.

'I suppose you've heard a certain amount about me from Dee Vaughan,' she began. 'I understand she and her husband know you. Are they "helping you with your enquiries", Inspector?'

'In a way, I suppose you could say that,' Graves agreed jovially. 'Taking an intelligent interest might be nearer the mark.'

'So you know that I was madly jealous of Miranda Travers, especially after she kissed Gabriel Field under the mistletoe, and I loathed her with a deadly loathing and am secretly delighted she's dead?'

'Please don't be sarcastic, Miss Bradley. It isn't helping matters.'

'All right, maybe that's an exaggeration, but I disliked the girl. Partly jealousy, I know—she was pretty and successful and sexy and young. But I genuinely disapproved of her, Inspector. She seemed like a…a sort of parasite—like that mistletoe. Feeding off other people, their admiration, their money… Oh, I know she earned her own living, but that was *fun* compared with what I go through every week! You don't stay young long with classes of London kids, year in, year out. And she was a gold digger all right. What about Robert Thornton, and then there was some rich Italian, wasn't there? And she couldn't keep her paws off

Gabriel and Terence Fitzgerald and even Barry Vaughan. If Tony Avery and the Major hadn't been totally immune to her she'd have added them to the list as well!'

'You sound as if you've a compulsion to confess, Miss Bradley,' Ken remarked drily. She raised defiant eyes to his level blue gaze and flushed slightly.

'Not to murder… I gather you think Miranda was killed by an overdose of her heart pills. Heavens, I didn't even know she *had* a heart condition till the rumours started flying a couple of hours ago! I would have thought it was equally likely she'd overdosed. Not on purpose, but if she was sozzled out of her mind. She used to knock back the whisky, did you know that? She had a bottle of Haig in her room—a big one.'

'How do you know that?' enquired the Detective Inspector casually. 'She didn't invite you in for girlish confidences, I take it.'

'Hardly.' Joyce looked a bit nonplussed. 'I suppose I must have seen it when the door was open,' she said at last.

'But you wouldn't normally have been on that floor, would you? Your room and Mr Field's are on the ground floor—right next to the ones the Sergeant and I are temporarily occupying.'

'True. Though I've been up to see the Major once or twice, and he's on the same floor. Honestly,

I can't remember. Someone may have told me—
Terence Fitzgerald perhaps.'

'Was he in the habit of having a tête-à-tête in
Miranda's room?' Graves was smoother than ever.

'I don't know. I'm sure he'd been there, though,
and I think he mentioned she was keen on the
whisky, like himself—with a laugh, you know.'

'You didn't ever see any pills lying round—perhaps if you went into the bathroom on that floor?'

Joyce shook her head. 'I did go in once, to go
to the loo, *en route* to the Major's room for a game
of cards. But I didn't see any pills. Just assorted
flannels and soap and a mug of toothbrushes. The
Vaughans and the Major used it, because their
rooms didn't have en suite bathrooms.'

'And I suppose you were sound asleep all Christmas night, too?'

'As a matter of fact, I was. I was feeling a bit
keyed up, and I didn't think I'd be able to sleep,
so I took a sleeping tablet, and ten minutes later I
was out cold. Nearly slept through breakfast, only
Gabriel came in and woke me.'

'So what was it,' Graves asked patiently, twisting a pencil round his hands and leaning back in a
laid-back manner, 'that you feel you have to confess to, if it isn't the murder of Miranda Travers?'

Joyce Bradley flushed again, deeper this time.

'I suppose you've heard by now about someone

twisting a scarf round Miranda's neck during the party games?'

'Yes, I have.'

'Well, that was me,' Joyce declared abruptly.

'I gather you also told Miranda she was going to die.'

The flush receded, leaving Joyce white again.

'Yes. I'm ashamed of myself. It was one of those sudden impulses...you see, I was so angry with her for fooling around with Gabriel, I mean, he can do what he wants, of course, he's a free agent, but Miranda had so many men already. I really felt at that moment that she deserved to die, and I wanted to give her a fright, maybe make her behave better...oh, I don't know. Anyway, I was the "body" in the game, so I was supposed to lie down behind the sofa and pretend to be dead. I was on my way there when I bumped into Miranda—I could tell it was her because of her scent, and I could just about see her blonde hair, too. The scarf was lying over the back of a chair, so I just grabbed it and got behind Miranda and put it round her neck and pulled, and put on a throaty sort of voice and...said it.'

'And then what?'

'Oh, I dropped the scarf and slipped off behind the sofa and lay down as the "body". Miranda was still gasping. I'm pretty sure she didn't know it was me. It's odd...' Joyce's voice became very thoughtful, '…I knew just what a murderer must feel like, at that moment. A sense of power—exhilarating in a horrible way. Then I wanted to laugh. And then I started to feel ashamed of myself, and hoped that no one would find out.'

'Yes,' agreed Graves, grimly. 'That's what the average murderer—if there is such a thing as an *average* murderer—certainly hopes. That no one will find out that he or she has done it. Which means that the death has to be presented as natural causes, or accident—or someone else has to take the rap.'

Joyce's mouth dropped open and she gulped, 'But…but I *didn't* kill Miranda Travers, Inspector. I swear it. You've got to believe me.'

Graves raised an eyebrow.

'Why?' Then, relenting, he said. 'Unless you are a good bit more devious than I think you are, Miss Bradley, I do believe you didn't do it. But uttering menaces isn't a nice thing to do either, you know—however much the other person needs a fright. Incidentally, Miranda Travers became engaged to Robert Thornton, the industrialist, on Christmas Day—he proposed to her after a long courtship, and she accepted. So if Miranda had been allowed to live, she might have become a useful and happy wife and mother.'

'Oh.' Joyce gulped again. 'I'm sorry,' she said

in a small voice. 'I'm not normally so vindictive. I'm truly sorry she's dead.'

'It's all right, Miss Bradley, you can go now. If you think of anything else that might be helpful, let me know, won't you?'

Joyce promised and escaped thankfully from the room.

'A bit hard on her, weren't you, sir?' Ian Anderson ventured hesitantly.

'Perhaps. Ian, did you notice one discrepancy?'

'Between what she and Fitzgerald said? Yes, sir. He made out he'd never been in the girl's room and she made out he had.'

'When I pressed her, she wasn't so sure and said that Fitzgerald had made some joking remark about Miranda being keen on the hard stuff—she might have said that to him herself, or told him about her whisky bottle without his ever being in her room. Still, it makes you think, Ian. I have a feeling Mr Terry Fitzgerald might not be telling the entire truth. Well, Grant seems to have flown the coop for the moment—we'll have to go to Rye to see him. Which leaves Avery.'

Anthony Avery was perhaps the most confident of the people Graves had seen. He had an insouciant manner which just missed being patronising by a hair's breadth, and sat easily in his chair with his arms crossed, as comfortably as if he were discussing the weather.

'I'm a little surprised to find a Yard man, no less, Inspector. I wouldn't have thought the death of one empty-headed little model would have warranted diverting you to East Sussex—especially over Christmas.'

'She may have been a nonentity to you, Mr Avery, but her fiancé Robert Thornton is not, and he pulled out the stops to get me assigned.'

'Really? How nice to have influence like that. Well, I wish you luck, Inspector, but I'm afraid I can't help you much. Miranda and I didn't exchange more than a few words while she was alive. I'm afraid I wasn't as susceptible to her charms as the other men were—my partner, Terry Fitzgerald, was far more her cup of tea. Any pretty face and he turns on the blarney. Also, I wasn't on the premises at the time of the…well, I suppose you'd call it "tragedy", though without wishing to sound *too* callous, I can think of a lot more tragic events in this hard old universe of ours.'

'Can you prove that?'

'My dear man, I wasn't here that whole *night*. And apparently the alarm in my room went off in the small hours, causing considerable annoyance all round, but several people can vouch for my absence.'

'Oh, I know that, Mr Avery, but it's a simple matter to set an alarm, you know, in advance, and you might very well have driven back to The

Grove. Also, we have reason to believe that there was someone in Miranda Travers' room that night—giving her good cause to stay there in spite of the noise of the alarm and not come out to investigate.'

Avery threw back his head and laughed. There was nothing but slight surprise, rapidly followed by pure amusement, on his classically regular features.

He would have made a good actor, thought Ken, feeling he was watching a performance. Which did not necessarily invalidate what Avery said. He seemed like one who played to the gallery as a matter of course.

'My dear Inspector Graves, what a wonderful scenario! I really do congratulate you! You mean Miranda and I were really madly attracted to each other and spent a night of passion in her room, after which I stole away to my shop and she expired. Or, consumed with jealousy of the rich Mr Thornton, I ordered her to give him up and, on her refusal, killed her—it was pills, wasn't it? Forced them down her, no doubt. Grand opera isn't it? Really, you'll have to do better than that.' His eyes gleamed sardonically as he added, 'In any case, I had a guest at my flat. She was the real reason I stole off from The Grove with what I admit was a rather lame excuse of having to work. Actually, we did work—some of the time. So you've been *cher-chez*-ing the wrong *femme*, dear Inspector!'

'I take it you can prove this?'

'Certainly. Jessica—her name is Jessica Downes—rang me at The Grove on Christmas Day and announced that she was motoring over from Bosham, where she was staying, and I could entertain her either here or at my flat in Rye, whichever I chose. Since I was bored here and I didn't fancy a night of French farce, with Jessica and I commuting from the first floor to the ground or top, where the vacant rooms were, and vice versa, I was off like a shot. The lady is still installed in my flat—she was there when the Vaughans paid a visit to the shop, on Boxing Day, on their way back from enlisting Robert Thornton. They didn't see her, though—they were only on the shop premises. Jessica can confirm all this, and since we were seen at various times by people in the street, and a neighbour, I imagine you'll believe her.'

And that, as Graves ruefully remarked to Sergeant Anderson, seemed to be that.

ELEVEN

A Spot of Breaking and Entering

Dee

BARRY RAISED his head from what appeared to be his fifth re-reading of the draft of *Framed Murder*.

'Mercury,' he said, in the far-away voice of one residing on some fluffy cloud far from terra firma.

Bella, crouched on the floor of our bedroom, raised her head. 'Woof,' she added hopefully. When Barry comes to life, or, indeed, shows any sign of life at all after a dormant period, Bella takes it as a hopeful sign, promising perhaps walkies, or, at any rate, a pat and cuddle or some signs of attention. But this time Barry was immune.

'Mercury,' he repeated, his voice this time distinctly contemplative. What you might call his *cogito ergo sum* voice. I lay back on the bed and waved one foot in the air. The pink-pearl lacquer on my toe-nails was proving slow to dry.

'Darling, far be it from me to interrupt your sessions of sweet silent thought, but what exactly do you mean by "Mercury"? Is it a code name, gasped out by the expiring MI5 man, or an observation on the contents of thermometers, or what? Or—wait a minute, I think I remember reading a novel once where mercury was used to murder somebody...'

Barry shook his head impatiently. 'Messenger of the Gods.'

'I know *that,* dear heart. But you're still not making yourself exactly clear.'

Barry sighed, straightened his back, and swivelled his chair round to face me.

'The figure I found in the desk in the back room at Avery Antiques was a Mercury. Bronze. Very fine.'

'*What* figure, light of my life?'

Barry glanced around uneasily at my saccharine tones. In moments of rare stress I have been known to hurl things at him. 'Well, it was like this,' he began...

'So you think it might be Miranda's statuette?' I concluded once he had finished.

'It might. But that's not all.' His brow remained furrowed in thought. Suddenly he said, 'Have you ever read "The Life of Benvenuto Cellini"?'

'Barry, you don't mean...?'

'Well, even if you have, I'll refresh your memory. Benvenuto, in the course of an eventful life— during which he was imprisoned and escaped in dramatic circumstances, fathered numerous children in and out of wedlock, and indulged in various fights with various people, being a hotheaded fellow—produced many beautiful things in the way of silversmithing, the most famous of which was the celebrated saltcellar with its symbolic representations of Sea and Land. He produced works for the Medici, various popes and cardinals and Francis I of France, living at his court for some time. Some of these works were statues or models for statues, since Cellini was a sculptor as well as a master craftsman.'

'Witness the Perseus in Florence,' I broke in.

'Exactly. In fact, he made a model of this in wax, in miniature, first. He would have made bronzes of small size as well as large-as-life sculptures, and indeed may well have copied some of them from wax models, as 'try-outs', intending to make larger statues later. The workmanship in each would have been perfect, as Cellini was a perfectionist, with a one-track mind as far as his craft and his reputation in his field went. Mythological figures like Perseus were a must in that day and age.'

I was beginning to feel vaguely excited, but tried to introduce a note of proper scepticism.

'Hold your horses, darling, don't you think you might just be reading a teeny bit too much into this?'

'Of course I might. It's probably just a flight of fancy, encouraged by our recent visit to Italy and my mugging up art and sculpture a bit for *Framed Murder*. Also, when I saw the bronze, I took it to be a nineteenth century one. But I do seem to recall reading somewhere, in an idle moment, in one of those glossies you get the gossip in, that Guido's family have various ancient tapestries, the occasional old master adorning the walls in the ancestral home—Peruginos and the like—lots of antique furniture, and some genuine Cellini bronzes. It came back to me suddenly,' he explained complacently. 'In the dentist, I think it was, I was reading the glossy—which was out of date,' he added censoriously.

'They always are in dentists.' I lowered my foot, which had remained in mid-air during this enthralling exposé. The lacquer was certainly dry by this time, even if I'd acquired cramp in the process. 'So what are you going to do about this interesting theory of yours?'

'Well, that's all it is, isn't it? A theory. Oh, I'll pass it on, for what it's worth, to Ken. In due course. After,' Barry concluded firmly, 'I have completed the next chapter of *Framed Murder*, which, as you are aware, has been sadly neglected. There are such things as publishers baying at one's heels, you know.'

Certainly, as far as Barry was concerned, the business of sleuthing had lost its immediate urgency with the sense of Ken Graves having taken over the reins. But I didn't feel quite the same way. For a start, I didn't have a novel to work on while penned up in The Grove. Secondly, I've never encountered a gen-u-ine non-museum Cellini at close quarters, or, indeed, any quarters, and after all I *am* an art-lover, as my holiday sessions over the years trailing round the Louvre, the Rijksmuseum, the Prado et al will attest. And finally, I am a woman. Enough said.

I allowed another quarter of an hour to elapse, during which I turned pages loudly and had two (manufactured) coughing fits. I am very familiar with Barry's back, and it was now expressing irritation.

'Darling, I think I'll just take Bella out for a stretch, then turn her in to Betty.' Bella's tail thumped approvingly. She was even more bored than I was. I expect Milton's daughters felt much the same way while the great man was composing, but just didn't dare to show it.

'Uuurrgh-ummm.' This vague sound signified approval.

'After that I think I'll take the Mini and have a bit of a runaround. Where are the keys?'

'In my jacket pocket. On the bed.' Barry hunched his shoulders and bent more closely over the escritoire. He didn't say, 'Getting a bit late, isn't it?' or something like that, designed to discourage, which he certainly would have done, if not in the throes.

I appropriated the keys, and Bella, and we had a brisk trot together round the garden, after which she was duly delivered to Betty. Wrapping my sheepskin jacket and woolly scarf more snugly round me, I got into the Mini and started it up.

'Heigh-ho, my doughty charger, my stalwart steed,' I murmured, patting its (cracked) upholstery. 'We're off to deeds of derring-do.'

I had not, at that precise moment, worked out exactly what my plan of campaign was to be. Secrecy was of the essence, but on the other hand there is such a thing as breaking and entering with intent…and I didn't like to think of the steely Newman-in-ice glint of Ken Graves' eyes if I should be discovered on a compromising situation. I would just have to hope, I decided as I bowled along merrily, that some bright idea would occur to me between now and Avery Antiques. It didn't.

I parked the car some distance away and Hush-Puppied along edgily to the corner of the shop. Avery Antiques was, as surmised, closed up for the evening, and, understandably, the side-entrance door was also closed. The upstairs part was quiet as the Western Front as well, with just a lamp gleaming its light behind drawn curtains to show human occupation. I thought I could hear the strains of the Brandenburg Concerto. Which, hopefully, might mask any sounds I was likely to make.

Sneaking along to the back of the building, I located the back office. It had a sash window, which was closed. However, after furtive glances round, further investigation showed that there was a hair's-breadth opening at the bottom. In the depths of the sheepskin jacket resided a whistle, a half-eaten bag of fudge, a torch, a lipstick, a lace-edged hanky—and the Swiss army knife, a present from Cousin Don after a visit to Geneva. I usually carry it round on expeditions. One never knows when a Swiss army knife will come in handy, even though this was the cut-price edition, *sans* gadget for removing stones from horses' hooves. Anyway, I inserted a trusty blade, and pushed upwards. The hair's-breadth crack enlarged. A few more tries, and I could insert my fingers, and push upwards with rather more force.

After that it was easy as pie. More furtive glances revealed no staring eyes, not even a cat's, and I was able to climb in over the window-sill and drop almost silently to the floor.

I paused to listen, but there was no sound from above—I couldn't even hear the Brandenburg Concerto, which presumably meant whoever was up there wouldn't be able to hear me either, unless I really started banging around. Nevertheless, my heart was beating uncomfortably. I'm a mere am-

ateur in the breaking and entering line, you understand.

Switching on the pencil torch, I moved over to
the Queen Anne bureau. This time, it *was* locked,
but I was in luck again—the key turned out to be
inside an inlaid cigar-box on the top of the bureau.
Naturally I looked there, because Barry and I keep
the key to the desk in a box like that, and people
do seem to repeat the same patterns of behaviour,
especially when it comes to concealing keys.
(Come to think of it, maybe we'd better move
ours!) By this time my heart had settled down, but
I was still prepared for disappointment.

But no. The tissue-paper-wrapped object was
still there, and as I unwrapped it carefully the paper
fell away to reveal a bronze figure of the god Mercury, a figure which in the light of my torch looked
so perfectly proportioned, so lovingly fashioned,
and so gloriously, heart-catchingly beautiful, so ex-
quisitely perfect, as to convince me it could very
well be a Cellini. I had a brief, feminine pang of
jealousy for the departed Miranda, whose beauty
could not only bewitch men but bewitch them into
wild, extravagant gestures like the gift of this statuette.

'Click!' There was a sound from the door, and
as I half-spun to face it, the turning handle turned
completely, and a hand reached in to switch on the
lights. I blinked owl-like, in the gush of radiance,

and stood stupidly, like an animal trapped in the rushing headlights of an oncoming car. Framed in the open doorway stood a woman. She was dark and slim and quite, quite gorgeous. One eyebrow was raised quizzically.

'And who,' she demanded, in what is usually described as a 'seductively husky' voice, 'are you?'

'Er-um,' I muttered.

Another figure appeared at the door. It was tall, its face wore a menacing expression, and it pointed a small automatic at me.

'Good evening, Mrs Vaughan.' The situation—down to the opened sash window behind me—was taken in in one sweeping glance.

'Without wishing to sound too banal, this is a most unexpected visit. Jessica, you take that—and hold onto it.' 'That' was the Mercury, which Jessica neatly whisked from my unresisting hand.

'I think we'd better continue this conversation in comfort and privacy upstairs, don't you?' Anthony Avery stood aside to let Jessica pass, then motioned to me to do the same. 'And don't try to get out into the street.'

I hadn't intended to. Unless one is completely desperate or supremely confident of success, I don't think it is a good idea to run with an automatic trained on one.

Obediently I trailed up the stairs after Jessica. Avery brought up the rear. A few seconds later I was ensconced in a white leather armchair in a living-room whose pristine Scandinavian lines could not have been more removed from the antiques downstairs. I stared at a Dali etching on the white wall beside me, as Anthony Avery perched on the arm of the white leather couch, idly shifting the gun from one hand to the other. He looked casual—but not too casual.

'Jessica, would you pour out drinks? Vodka and tonic, Martini, gin and orange, Campari, Southern Comfort, Scotch on the rocks, bourbon-and-water—or just plain sherry, Mrs Vaughan?'

'Dee, please,' I said automatically, then gulped. It was not, after all, your conventional social occasion. 'Southern Comfort.'

I needed comfort. The Mercury was now standing on top of a pale wood cabinet, while Jessica dispensed drinks onto a pewter tray. He looked out-of-place, as a knight on horseback might have looked trotting around a modern Ring Road. But still beautiful.

Jessica brought over the drinks. She moved with infinite grace, but a sinuous panther-type grace rather than the grace of delicacy, counteracting the previous impression produced by her silence and unquestioning response to Avery's orders. Her dress was long, black velvet and cut to cling and then flare out gradually to the hem. She wore a diamond, pear-shaped, round her neck, suspended from a silver chain and nestling in her cleavage. No earrings or rings, and her hair was swept back smoothly behind her exquisitely-shaped ears, and then left running loose down her back. Her skin was startlingly white, her brows, hair and eyes startlingly black.

Shakespeare's Rosaline, or the Dark Lady of the Sonnets, I thought, with her black 'pitch-ball eyes'. And when we had all taken our drinks she paused for a moment with hers behind Anthony and ran her fingers caressingly over the back of his neck. I could sense the electricity between them as she curled up on the sofa, resting her elbow on his knee, and turned a long swan-neck to look long and consideringly at me.

'And now you're going to tell us what you were doing with our Mercury,' she said, her husky voice taking over control of the situation. I had a feeling there weren't many situations she couldn't take control of. No wonder Anthony had been impervious to the charms of Miranda Travers, when he had his own Cleopatra waiting in the background.

'Yes, that would be rather a good idea.' Anthony's voice was mocking. 'Did you come after that item in particular—in which case, how did you know where to find it? Or was this just a spot of general burglary?'

'For a start,' I said briskly, 'I'm not a thief, as I'm sure you know very well. Secondly, my husband found the statuette when we visited your shop previously—he came across it by chance when poking round aimlessly in the office waiting for us. Thirdly, he knows where I am [untrue] and Detective Inspector Graves, whom we happen to know rather well, will be making enquiries if I don't turn up in time for late dinner at The Grove—so you might as well stop playing with that gun. And fourthly, it's not *your* Mercury. I'm pretty confident it's Miranda Travers' Mercury, at one remove from the di Montefalcone's Umbrian castle. So, to take the ball into your court, Anthony, how come you're in possession of it? It was rather stupid to remove it, wasn't it—though I can't credit you actually killed for it. No, not even for a Cellini.'

I heard an intaken breath then, and Jessica leaned forward.

'It's not a Cellini,' she said baldly.

'No?' I managed to imply polite scepticism.

'No.'

'Jessica,' explained Avery almost absently, 'is a sculptress and something of an art expert as well. She valued Renaissance objects for Christie's at one time.'

'Oh.'

I must have managed to imply scepticism in that monosyllable, because Jessica darted me an antagonistic glance, shrugged impatiently and got up, leaving the room suddenly.

Avery smiled. 'She's brilliant as well as beautiful,' he informed me. 'A truly Elizabethan type.'

'Perhaps. I don't exactly see her as the Barbara Hepworth type, though.'

'Oh, Jessica does very little in the way of large sculptures. More the size of Mercury here.'

'And she really worked for Christie's?'

'For about a year only—but you could verify it by ringing and asking for their Renaissance expert. He knows her.'

I glanced at Mercury poised on top of the cabinet. Granted, I had reacted ecstatically to him on discovery, but how much of that reaction was preconditioned, based on the belief that he had been produced in the workshop of the renowned Benvenuto? He still looked beautiful to me, but then, though something of an art enthusiast myself, I would find it extremely difficult to distinguish between an original and a good copy. It required training and the right eye to catch the subtle vibes. Or else the inborn instinct that makes the rare 'divvie'.

Jessica returned, as silently as she had disappeared, and sauntered languidly over to me.

'Here.' She held out a catalogue. It was for an exhibition at a Bond Street gallery of the sculptures of Jessica Downes, with photographs of three of the choicer pieces—an abstract on a marble plinth, a leaping puma and a group of dancers, captured in poses which I recognised from the last act of a specially-choreographed modern ballet based on ancient myths in twentieth-century stories. Jessica's photo was there, too, her lips wreathed with a faint Mona Lisa smile.

'I can't prove my credentials as an ex-valuer for Christie's, but you could check it easily enough.'

'Yes, so Anthony has told me.' They exchanged glances. She was holding a large brown envelope, which she also held out to me.

'This went with the Mercury—if you'd looked around in the bureau a bit longer, you'd have found it. You see, Miranda *lent* the Mercury to Anthony. She knew a real Cellini would fetch an enormous amount of money and she was afraid Guido would demand his Mercury back if she decided to marry someone else. If it was gone, she reasoned that though he might have a case for demanding at least part of the proceeds back, she could fight it on the grounds that it was a bona fide gift and, even if she lost, he couldn't recover what she had already spent as long as it wasn't on recoverable items. However, she was so much of an egotist that she believed without question that someone would hand over an immensely valuable item like a Cellini just on the strength of her pretty face.'

'And Guido didn't.'

'That's right. Oh, the di Montefalcone family do own the Cellini Mercury, but this is just a rather good nineteenth century copy—the nineteenth century being a heyday for bronzes. Anthony realised that it couldn't be the original when he found that the provenance—these documents in the envelope—was just photocopies of the true provenance for the original Cellini. In other words, Guido wanted to impress Miranda with the grand gesture, but it turned out to be a cut-price gesture after all. This Mercury is probably worth three thousand or so—a nice little sum but nothing like the vast amount a real Cellini would fetch.'

Avery took up the tale. 'Miranda couldn't resist telling Terry about the Mercury, and he told me. Miranda and I weren't exactly friendly, but I managed to pay her a visit in her room—*not* the famous night of the alarm, I hasten to add, I was genuinely here then, with Jessica. It was earlier on. We had a chat and when she heard about Jessica she agreed that Jessica would be the best person to middle-woman a sale, with all her contacts and the Christie connection. For a percentage, of course. She handed the Mercury and documents over to me, and I signed a receipt, which no doubt is somewhere among her effects. And I brought the whole caboodle round here. When Jessica turned up we went through the documents and Jessica pronounced it a copy. A disappointment, but we'd still have got a 10% commission on the sale of the copy, if Miranda decided to sell. Or, preferably, she'd have sold it to us. These things appreciate enormously, as you know, and in a few years its value would at least have doubled.'

It was all so glib. I now believed the story of the Mercury being a nineteenth century copy, but still felt suspicious of this pair. My vibes, which had remained dormant when confronted with Mercury, screamed out that they were partners in *some* wheeler-dealing escapade, even if innocent of murder.

'Why didn't you give the Mercury back, after Miranda's death?' I demanded. My suspicious frown was met with blandly innocent smiles.

'Well, we haven't had much time, have we? If you think we had plans to make off with it, you can think again. If it *had* been a genuine Cellini, Miranda would just have got Guido onto it—which explains why she was so trusting handing it over with just a receipt for proof, by the way. She made no bones about explaining that to me. Rather hurtful, really.'

'No honour among dealers, eh?' I was being nasty.

Anthony gave me a reproachful look. 'And if you think,' Jessica Downes interposed, at her most feline silky, 'that we would have murdered Miranda even for a real Cellini, you can think again. Everything would have pointed to us, so it would have been stupid, and the di Montefalcones would have set up a vendetta or something against us. Besides, neither Anthony nor I are poor, so we would hardly have risked a life sentence for such rich pickings. No,' she added thoughtfully, beating a tattoo on a tabletop with slender white fingers, 'someone else, someone *completely* different, is indicated.'

'Would you care to expand on that statement?' I enquired politely. But Jessica just gave a throaty laugh and raised an eyebrow.

'Not particularly. I have my own job—I don't intend to do the police's for them. If they're any good they'll get there sooner or later anyway.'

I thought of saying something sententious like 'It can be dangerous to conceal information', but I could imagine the carelessly mocking reaction that would get from Ms Downes, so I didn't.

'You looked at these, didn't you?' I nodded. 'Good—so you've seen for yourself that they're photocopies.' She neatly twitched the envelope back from me.

'Aren't you going to give them back—and the Mercury?' I demanded, as they both surveyed me ironically.

'Who to?' demanded Avery. 'Look, if the police require them as evidence, they're welcome to pick them up. But unless they've got a bearing on Miranda Travers' death, they're not evidence, are they? If Mercury was the real McCoy, obviously di Montefalcone would want him back, but I can't see him quibbling about a mere three-thousand worth. Presumably Mercury now forms part of Miranda's estate, thus going to whoever inherits her effects—her parents, I imagine. And I still want to buy Mercury. I shall merely wait a decent while—say, two weeks—then write explaining matters and putting in an offer. I'm sure they'll accept. With so much else on their minds, they'll hardly be bothered over this.'

It was callous but true, and no more callous than people conning old ladies to sell antiques at a third of their real value. There really wasn't much I could do, except tell Ken Graves of the whereabouts of the Mercury and hope he'd insist on taking charge of it. And, compared with finding Miranda's murderer, the matter of the Mercury was relatively unimportant.

Avery glanced at his watch.

'Presumably you drove here, Dee. Well, if you start off now, you'll be back at The Grove for dinner. You don't want another drink? No, well, perhaps not, if you're driving.'

He steered me firmly to the door of the flat. 'You can find your own way down, can't you? If you feel any further urge for exploration of the premises coming on, please resist it. I assure you we have no skeletons in the closet or Old Masters in the cupboards.'

An unkind ripple of laughter came from Jessica

Downes. The pitch-ball eyes watching me were amused.

'Sarky creatures,' I thought furiously, and wrenched my arm free of Anthony's.

'I can manage by myself perfectly well, thank you.' He leaned over the bannisters and watched me descend.

'Don't bang the side-door when you go out.'

Obviously he had judged my mood correctly. I glared back up from the bottom, to see him return into the flat, closing the door firmly behind him.

Pausing for a while to get my breath—and calm my temper—I suddenly got vibes. Up there, I was convinced, a conversation was going on which was important. Going to the side door I banged it, waited for the reverberations to cease shaking the house, and softly opened it again, leaving it on the latch. I then took off my Hush Puppies, put them as a wedge in the door, and crept up the stairs, which, I had noted the first time up, were the non-creaky kind. I stood outside the door and listened.

'So what was he doing driving over from Bosham the night of Miranda's death?' demanded the husky tones of Jessica Downes. 'I tell you, I *know* his car and I know him by sight too, quite well. After all, I do live part of the year there myself, in the cottage, and he's often there for weekends visiting the old man. If there isn't something very fishy about it, I'd be surprised. Why didn't he come forward and say?' There was a murmur in reply, then Jessica spoke again, scornfully.

'You're too chicken, Anthony. I tell you, I want the big-time. If we're not able to get hold of the Mercury now and pass it off as the genuine thing to our interested party, I want some compensation.' Another murmur, obviously expostulatory, from Avery, and another fierce retort from Jessica.

'Oh, don't be such an imbecile, Anthony. I don't mean anything crude and obvious—just a ''we're all in this together'' approach, and a suggestion of, perhaps, a partnership in another shop, with him putting up capital. After all, it would be a good investment for him...'

Dee, you're getting into deep waters here, I told myself. I didn't stay to hear more. My heart was beating just as hard now as when I did my spot of breaking and entering. I didn't think they'd hear the slight click of the side door as I pulled it shut this time. Especially as the first notes of a Mozart opera were now tinkling out from above—presumably as a soothing background for their less innocent plotting. Still, I didn't feel really safe till at least halfway back to The Grove. I missed the reassuring snuffles of Bella. The Lone Ranger, feeling very lone—that was me. Jessica Downes might not have actually committed a murder, but if ever I saw a potential killer, it was she. However, I doubted if she'd put anything over on Robert Thornton. I needed advice badly.

'HOW DID you get on with the manuscript, Barry?' I asked, over *sole bonne femme* and cucumber salad, with *duchesse* potatoes. In spite of all the upset, the cuisine at The Grove was back on form.

'Very well, thanks. A whole two chapters, and I should think I'll easily be able to finish it off in the Easter break, if not before. Do you want to hear what happened next?'

'Yes, please,' I lied, giving my wifely smile. Barry, bless him, was looking his most enthusiastically endearing, and it would have been like taking a rattle from a baby to say no.

'It's complex enough, don't you think?' he wound up, over Pavlova and coffee.

'Oh, yes,' I agreed, thinking that what had transpired that evening was even more so.

'Did you have a nice runaround in the car? Surely you weren't driving all that time—no, you couldn't possibly have been.'

'I stopped off somewhere,' I conceded. 'In fact, I've had quite an eventful time. I'll tell you about it when we go to bed.'

TWELVE

On the Trail

Barry

I WAS RATHER gratified to find from Dee that my instant placing of the Mercury as a nineteenth century bronze had been right. Maybe all that research for *Framed Murder* has paid off, and I am developing a genuine 'feel' for art. The other thing was of all my half-jokingly proffered hypotheses, that of Robert Thornton driving over and subsequently dotting his fiancée one seemed to be indicated as correct—or at any rate likely.

We had discussed the events of the previous evening until into the small hours. Dee fell asleep before me (hardly surprising, after all the wear and tear she'd been through, not to mention the physical effort of climbing through a window and so forth). I lay awake for a further hour, pondering. Mainly on the possible motive of Robert Thornton. The green-eyed monster was indicated, obviously—but what exactly had Miranda *done* to enrage him to such a degree? Especially since he hadn't been on

the spot to witness her flirtations. To my mind there
was only one possible solution—well, one that
seemed possible to me, anyway. But I wanted to
test out the hypothesis this time, before Dee or I
made any further move.

We ordered breakfast in our room, for once, feeling that it was best to continue our previous night's
discussion at once, in peace and privacy, while yesterday's discoveries were still 'hot off the press',
so to speak.

'I'm rather intrigued,' Dee murmured indis-
tinctly, through toast dripping with butter, 'by Jessica's reference to the Mercury and "an interested
party". Surely she didn't mean Robert, though she
did indicate she was looking to him, through some
sort of blackmail, for "compensation".'

'I'd find it easier to follow your thought processes, Dee, if you waited to swallow your toast,'
I complained.

'Sorry.'

'Granted.' I gave the matter due consideration.
'From what you said, they wanted to get hold of
the Mercury with probably some idea of palming
it off as a genuine Cellini after all.'

'But how? After all,' Dee objected, 'the proof of
provenance consisted of photocopies. The original,
together with the Cellini Mercury, is fast in the possession of the di Montefalcones in Umbria.'

'Yes, but with the photocopies, it wouldn't be

too difficult to find someone schooled in these matters to forge a very convincing version of the original, on old parchment, with processes for making the ink look faded and ancient as well.'

'I hadn't thought of that.'

'And,' I continued, warming to the theme, 'we've all read stories in which avid and none too scrupulous art collectors in the States and elsewhere will pay a small fortune in order to be able to gloat in private over a big-name work of art. Some of them have been ''done'' in the process, and serve them right. Jessica Downes seems to be the rash type who'll wade in where angels fear to tread, so it'd be the kind of gamble which would appeal to her. Added to which her say-so as an accredited Christie's assistant specialising in Renaissance works would be a great help.'

Dee nodded. 'It's feasible, certainly. I don't suppose said collector would contact the di Montefalcones.'

'If he did, Guido would hardly blow the gaff, since it would be an embarrassment to him to be exposed as the kind of cheapskate who fobs his girl off with cheap copies.'

Dee giggled. 'The artistic equivalent of the rhinestone brooch. Sort of.'

'Precisely. On a far more sumptuous scale.'

Dee topped up our coffee cups again.

'It must,' she remarked thoughtfully, 'have been

the most awful shock for Anthony and Jessica when we blew in on the scene.'

'Yes, but unless you called their bluff and got Ken Graves to confiscate Mercury as part of the evidence—difficult—nothing much has been changed. Even if you did, it would have to be returned to Miranda's family in due course, and unless someone else got in with a better offer, the way would be clear for Avery Antiques to make a bid. After that, who would be interested in its subsequent fate, especially if they held onto it for a year or so before disposing of it to the "interested party"? No,' I continued, sipping the coffee and puckering my brows in thought, 'if Jessica really did see Thornton's Mercedes beetling over in this direction the night of Miranda's demise—or rather, the night before her demise, strictly speaking, as it was the morning—then *he* must have been the one who had a shock when we two suddenly arrived earnestly demanding justice.'

'No wonder he quoted Webster. Psychological give-away.'

'Yes, and that Browning stuff appears to have been hit-on. But what I've been cudgelling my brains about while you were snoring away...'

'I do *not* snore!' came an indignant squeak.

'While you were breathing evenly through your delicate nostrils,' I agreed equably, 'is the why and the wherefore. And the only satisfactory conclusion

I came up with is that instead of *accepting* him when he proposed over the phone on Christmas Day, she turned him down.'

'Perhaps he didn't propose at all, and it's all a cover story.'

'No, I imagine he did. You see, the courtship had been so public, and that kind of man can't bear to be made to look a fool. Besides, she may have insulted him unbearably in some way.'

'Deriding his deficiencies as a lover, you mean, or something like that?'

'Possibly. Or maybe even announcing she was throwing him over for someone totally unsuitable— like Gabriel Field or Morgan Grant.'

'Yes, I don't imagine the charming Guido would have been in favour after Tony and Jessica exposed his trick with the Mercury. Even if at the time she planned to join them in their scam.'

I removed the breakfast tray and stood up.

'Nick and Nora time again. Action!'

'Er—exactly *what* action, Barry?' Dee demanded, as I backed the Mini out of the driveway of The Grove with a flourish. Inside, Ken Graves and his aide-de-camp were doing what a policeman's gotta do.

'They gotta do more if I'm right, and soon,' I declared.

'Barry, what *are* you on about?' My longsuffering spouse raised her eyes to Heaven. 'Sometimes I wonder. And *where* are we going?'

'The Telephone Exchange. *Someone* will have been on duty on Christmas morning. And probably not feeling very happy about it. Bored, no doubt.'

Light dawned. 'You mean someone might have listened in to Robert Thornton's call to Miranda?'

'Might. It's a long shot, of course, but it's not beyond the bounds of possibility. I want to try and check this out if possible before approaching Ken with our story. But I think it requires the tactful approach. We are "helping the police with their enquiries", by the way.'

'Of course we are. Was that ever in doubt?'

MOST PEOPLE have had the experience of their phone calls being listened into by switchboard operators. It's an infringement of privacy, downright annoying and sometimes can be embarrassing—at least it would be if one were aware at the time that one's every fatuity is being hung on. My hunch, miraculously, proved to be right, as proved by a lively-looking kid with snapping eyes and a ring on her engagement finger. The kind who would certainly be sharing a flat in London with three or four more of her ilk if she hadn't been doing overtime in Sussex saving for the mortgage with a local lad.

A few admiring glances and a little something towards the mortgage from me, and some artless

girl-to-girl tactful chatter from Dee, and we were
well away, initial hostility thawed. Yes, Robert
Thornton had put through a call to The Grove, to
Miss Travers, on Christmas morning. In fact, it had
been the only one of two calls during her shift, the
other being from an anxious father-to-be to a hos-
pital. Yes, he'd seemed to be proposing marriage,
all right, but in rather a brusque 'Come on, isn't it
about time we settled the date?' kind of way. The
lady hadn't taken too kindly to that, and 'said she'd
be damned if she'd be hurried, and he said he'd
had enough of dancing to her tune, and she said
there were other fish in the sea, and he said she
wouldn't find better than him with all he had to
offer, so he advised her to think again—quickly.'

'Shades of *My Last Duchess* and the ''centuries'
old name'',' murmured Dee to me. 'Except it isn't
centuries old.'

On cue, the girl Lynne continued her saga. 'She
said marriage wasn't a bargain basement and it
didn't matter how much money he had, he'd never
be a gentleman. His manners showed his origins
and she wasn't going to be ordered about by a dom-
ineering brute of a fellow and she wasn't going to
spend her life putting up with the advances of
someone who had about as much subtlety as a bad-
tempered bull. What's more, he wasn't even *fun*,
he was a bore; the only fun she'd ever have out of
him would be breaking the engagement as publicly

as possible and making a laughingstock of him, and she rather thought she would, too; and the gossip columns would have a field day, just right for the slack after-Christmas period, added to which his business practices weren't above question...'

At that point, apparently, Thornton had told her he was coming over to discuss the matter with her rationally (but he sounded furious) 'and she said he didn't know what rationally meant, and *he* said she'd better be ready to see him that night—he was tied up till then—and he'd storm the place unless she agreed to let him in quietly. She gave a giggle and said well, if he wanted a quiet session she'd give him another chance, and he could get in by the French windows in the drawing-room which she'd leave ajar and told him how to find them. So it sounded as if they'd sort of made it up...' But Lynne's voice was a bit dubious.

We thanked her copiously, received her assurance that she'd be willing to repeat all this before the police if necessary, and that in the meantime she faithfully promised not to divulge a word, and set off back to The Grove.

'It's hearsay evidence,' I mused, as hedges and fields sped by.

'Yes—so's what I heard Jessica telling Tony Avery.' We sighed in unison.

'Talking of that, from what you tell me, Jessica

Downes doesn't seem to be the kind of girl to let the grass grow under her feet.'

'I would say the grass has very little chance of survival under her feet.'

'So what's the betting she and Avery will be off pretty *pronto* to Redditch Grange to ask what Thornton's Merc was doing in the long, dark drive to East Sussex?' We gazed at each other with a wild surmise.

'Do you think he'll let anything slip?'

'I don't think he'll deny it—Jessica would know him well by sight, from what she said, as well as his car. He'll probably deny killing Miranda.'

'Maybe he didn't.'

'Maybe not, but he was certainly on the spot, though we don't know yet whether it was at the relevant time.'

'I think,' Dee said slowly, 'it's time we spilt the beans to Ken Graves.'

'I think possibly you're right.'

But when we got into The Grove, I headed straight for the telephone directories in the downstairs lobby, and the phone.

'Now what, Barry?'

'Just checking something.' Sure enough, the phone at Avery Antiques rang and rang unanswered—which it shouldn't have done, because Christmas was over and it was back-to-business time.

'Dee,' I said, 'I'm going to leave you to give the explanations to Ken in your own inimitable way. I'm off again.'

'Let me guess—Redditch Grange?'

'Where else?'

'Where else indeed? I'm coming too.'

'Someone,' I pointed out, 'has to give the facts to the fuzz. And you had your slice of the action last time—it's my turn now.' There's one thing I'll say for my wife—she's usually fairminded.

'OK. But Barry, be careful. They're all three pretty ruthless characters. What are you going to *do*, anyway?'

'I don't know yet, exactly,' I confessed. 'Skulk around and try and get some evidence that isn't hearsay, and wait for you to bring in the Marines.'

'Auf Wiedersehen then.'

'Ciao to you too.'

Before I left The Grove yet again, I dashed up to the bedroom and got two things: my duffel-coat with the deep pockets, and my small portable tape-recorder. I sometimes use this to dictate the current opus into, but recently I've found the flow comes more easily on the type-writer, or even with the old pen-and-paper method, so it had a new and unused cassette, as I'd done whatever writing I did at the escritoire since being here.

The progress of this case seemed to be depending very much on overheard conversations—Jessica's to Anthony Avery and Thornton's Christmas call (via the switchboard girl) to Miranda. It was unlikely Thornton would spill the gaff to me, or in front of me, so, boringly repetitive as it was getting to be, I was just going to have to depend on snooping again. If I could get anywhere near them. And this time I'd try to get a record of what was said.

THE TROUBLE with a place like Redditch Grange is that there's absolutely no way of approaching the house in total secrecy. I did my best, parking the Mini around a corner up the road, outside the hedges of a half-timbered mock-Tudor mansion. I then made my way up the gravelled drive of Redditch Grange, as close to the side hedge and as far from eye-shot of the front windows as I could. No cry of 'Halt, stranger!' met my ears, but I couldn't swear I hadn't been seen by some aged retainer. Something told me the smooth Tony Avery would have demanded privacy for the interview (yes, he *was* there, with or without the Dark Lady of the Sonnets, as Dee had described her—his BMW was in evidence in the driveway next to the Merc). So probably they'd be in a room at the back of the Grange somewhere, not the morning-room Dee and I had been shown into.

Thanking Providence that it was still winter, albeit an exceptionally fine winter, and that therefore no swooping flocks of gardeners would be in evidence, I continued my skulking crab-like motion round the corner of the house. Now, here came the difficult part. I would be just as visible to anyone looking out of any of the windows as they would be to me looking in.

'Luck, be a lady tonight,' I breathed, disregarding the fact it was nowhere near night. And she was. The first window I came to at the back looked in to a small study. It had diamond-paned casement windows, one slightly ajar. It also had Anthony Avery and Robert Thornton facing each other across the room—antagonistically to judge by their stances—and a dark-haired woman seated in an easy chair, her legs stretched out in front in an obtrusively relaxed way. All three were profile from the window, which was all to the good, as long as I was there.

I took the tape-recorder from my pocket and switched it on to full volume. Cautiously I pushed it round the edge of the opened window and under the overhanging curtain, not enough to muffle the sound, but enough to partly conceal it. It wasn't large—it should stay there safely unless one of them decided to walk over to the window to close it or open it further. And there was half an hour's recording on that cassette. The main problem was, had everything, or nearly everything significant, already been said before my arrival? And that I wouldn't know unless I found out that they'd only just arrived ahead of me.

I edged my way round the side of the house, along the hedge and out of the open gates. Then I walked round to the Mini and parked myself in it to watch the main road and the arrival of the troops.

THIRTEEN

Approaching the End

Barry

THE TROOPS did turn up, Robert Thornton agreed to accompany the police for questioning, and Avery and Jessica were detained separately. My cassette recorder was salvaged too.

'It was a good idea, Barry,' Ken Graves said sympathetically. 'But it hasn't really added anything. Never mind,' he added placatingly, 'who knows, it *could* have provided vital information.'

We'd been allowed to listen to the tape. It ran for about fourteen minutes after I'd placed it, by which time Ken & Co had arrived on the scene. Part of that time was spent in stony silence. During the rest, Thornton repeatedly declared his innocence, while admitting he had driven over to The Grove. Jessica, who herself had started off in her car very late, had seen him round midnight, but, according to Thornton, he had driven around country lanes for a while, then parked near a farmhouse to have a smoke and think out what he was going to say to Miranda. He had decided that he'd made a mistake, and that marriage was now just not on— the problem was, how to resolve it amicably and prevent Miranda doing yet another volte-face and deciding she wanted him after all. Many cigarettes later he had realised how late it was, but pressed on, parking the Mercedes some distance from The Grove and walking to the hotel, where he found the French window ajar as Miranda had promised. Knowing her room number, he found it without difficulty and, as the door was unlocked, let himself in.

There had been no sound from any of the other rooms, and Miranda had explained about the alarm going off, saying that everyone had obviously dropped off to sleep again afterwards, dead tired after the Christmas junketings and the unexpected interruption to their slumbers. She herself just hadn't bothered to appear on the landing, confident that sooner or later someone or other would switch the damned thing off without her arrival on the scene being necessary.

She had by this time given him up and was surprised when he appeared at her room. Both of them were in a sober, rational mood, the tempers of the morning's phone conversation put behind them, and they agreed that the best thing was to call the marriage plans off.

At this point Graves stopped the tape and explained that, in questioning, Robert Thornton had conceded that he had offered Miranda a settlement, in the form of a large cash or jewellery gift, if she agreed to the parting of the ways with maximum discretion. He had warned her that he had no intention of upping the offer. Of course, as Graves gloomily remarked, all this could be true or false, and Thornton was still prime suspect.

The rest of the tape conversation was somewhat more interesting. Miranda, according to Thornton, had said she didn't want to marry anyone yet, but had hinted with some smugness at a new relationship with someone she 'was in a deal with' who was 'sexy, full of fun and made her feel fulfilled as a woman and a person'. Thornton had rather coldly wished her joy of it, and Miranda had said that she wouldn't mind marrying him, although he had no money to speak of. She had offered Thornton whisky, to celebrate their release from each other and to toast her new lover, still un-named. Thornton had refused, and Miranda had said something like, 'Oh, all right, it's time for beddy-byes now, and Miranda will drink up her cocoa instead like a good little girl.' She'd drained some cocoa from a flask, remarking it didn't taste very nice and maybe she'd have the whisky as well.

By this time Thornton, anxious to be on his way, moved to the door, telling her he'd be in contact and warning her once again to be discreet. He said he'd got as far as the drawing-room when he heard her coming along behind him. She staggered into the room, spluttering, her face livid, and just managed to grab hold of him before she collapsed. They went down together, she striking her head against the side of a table. Then her fingers relaxed and once he had extricated himself and got a good look at her, he realised she was dead, though he tested pulse and breathing to make sure. By this time, awakening to the awkward situation he was in, his one thought was to get out, which he did, wiping the handle of the French window of his prints as he went.

'All this tallies with what he told us,' Ken said, 'only he gave a good deal of detail about his feelings and how he's aware this doesn't show him in a very good light, but someone in the public eye always has to think of their image, and a lot of gumph like that.'

'One can see why Miranda wanted out,' Dee observed. 'And he *is* a ruthless type.'

'One can also see why he wanted out,' I said drily.

'Oh, granted.'

The tape tailed off into vituperation after that, with Thornton accusing Avery and Jessica of blackmail and stating he would repeat everything he had just told them to the police, they had nothing on him, and what's more, he wouldn't put it past Av-

ery to have poisoned Miranda's cocoa ahead of
time, arranging for the alarm to go off so he'd have
the perfect alibi. He was accusing Avery of being
Miranda's new fancyman when Graves arrived and
the tape finished off its recording in a confused
babble of voices. The rest was silence.

'Presumably Thornton denied touching the flask,
let alone washing it out and leaving it clear of
prints,' I said.

'Correct.'

'Either he's lying, or someone else (the guilty
party, presumably) got into Miranda's room and
washed out the evidence before there was any hue
and cry.'

'Obviously.'

'Did you get anything out of Anthony and Jessica?'

'Not much. They repeated the tale of Miranda
lending them the bronze for valuation, and indignantly denied any nefarious purpose in connection
with the Mercury other than buying it from Miranda's heirs, waiting for its value to increase, and
selling it at a profit. All good clean business prac-
tice. Nothing to prove otherwise, and Miranda's
vague talk of a ''deal'' could have referred to anything with anyone.'

'It was obviously the Major's capsules,' I pon-
dered aloud. 'The murderer opened them and put
the powered contents into the cocoa. The digitoxin,

taken on top of Miranda's previous digitalis medication, produced a fatal heart attack shortly after the cocoa had been drunk. The poor kid must have just about been able to stagger down the stairs after Thornton, the only person awake and able to assist her. She probably realised there had been something in the cocoa, but might not have realised she was just on the point of death.'

Dee shuddered. 'Did she realise who had doctored the cocoa, I wonder?'

'I doubt it,' I considered. 'Melodramatic as it seems, I think she'd have found the strength to gasp it out to Thornton. After all, she managed to get down the stairs and to clutch onto him.'

'It could all be a massive double-bluff,' Graves pointed out, his blue eyes gleaming keenly. 'Thornton could have gone into the bathroom, seen the Major's capsules and read the description on the label. He's a quick thinker, used to acting fast and taking risks. Also, as her long-term suitor, he was more likely to know of Miranda's heart condition and medication than anyone here. He could have pocketed the capsules and waited for a suitable moment to introduce them into the cocoa, or maybe into an alcoholic drink, but the cocoa was better for his purposes.'

'Yes, but if he was driving round and parking for a smoke and sessions of not-so-sweet silent thought, as he stated, and arrived well *after* the digital-alarm incident, it'd all have to be a rush job, and I fail to see why he should go into the bathroom on our floor when it was dark and he didn't want to attract attention and Miranda had a perfectly good en suite bathroom complete with loo anyway.'

'I take your point about the bathroom,' Ken sighed. 'As to the timing, again it's his word. He could well have arrived before the alarm incident and have been in her room during it, providing a very good reason why she didn't appear. I thought his explanation of her non-appearance suspiciously pat. Of course, it's possible that someone at or near the farmhouse he claims to have parked outside might be able to substantiate his claim that he was there when he said he was. I'm having it checked out.'

'Let's face it,' Dee pointed out, 'Robert Thornton's the only one we've come up with who appears to have anything like an adequate motive, and we've only his word for a lot of things, including the fact that he and Miranda made peace in the wee small hours.' Dee is strong on motive. 'Don't you agree, Barry?'

'No,' I said flatly. 'It's all too pat and streamlined. And Thornton may have a temper, but he really means all that about a man in his position, and in a way he's right. I think he was uncharacteristically stupid in arranging to come over here at night for a secret meeting with Miranda, as he obviously realised when he was sitting smoking and pondering in the car. He'd have been well advised to turn back and drive to Bosham, but either because, having given his word he didn't want to go back on it, or, more likely, he didn't want to enrage Miranda into phoning the Daily Blab or whatever first thing in the morning, he gritted his teeth and got on with it. He'd obviously realised late in the day that Miranda Travers was the last person suitable to be his wife—apart from being incompatible she did, from his point of view, turn out to be most unstable. I think it was in character for him to offer her some financial inducement to be discreet and keep a low profile for a while—enough time for him to pick out another and more suitable beauty to squire.'

'It's a pity,' Dee sighed, 'that Miranda didn't actually tell him the name of her new beau. I suppose it couldn't have been Guido all the time?'

'Hardly. Thornton knew about Guido. It wasn't a "new relationship". The only "deal" we know about is Miranda's agreement with Avery about the Mercury, and, given Miranda's obvious fondness for money, it's highly possible she was willing to go in with Avery and Jessica in passing the Mercury off as a Cellini to a foreign buyer.'

'Barry, really!' Dee snorted. 'I buy the deal part of it, but do you really see Miranda falling for Anthony's smooth charms? I know all that stuff about hostility being the basis of sexual attraction, and Anthony might just about have had time to seduce Miranda in the brief time he was here, but I can't believe it. Added to which, *La Primavera,* the Dark Lady of the Sonnets and Tony Avery make a most unlikely *ménage à trois!*'

KEN GRAVES stood up reluctantly.

'I've still got Thornton, Avery and Downes in custody in Rye, but I'm going to have to release them soon. Carry on regardless, you two—and tell me when you've solved it, won't you? Concrete proof,' he added wistfully, 'would be nice.'

'Hold on, Dee,' I protested, as the door closed behind Ken, and we returned to the problem like two dogs worrying a bone. 'What I said was "the only deal we know about". She could have had another going, for all we know. And I'm inclined to agree about Avery. I can see Miranda being inveigled into a questionable, even criminal venture with him, if the stakes were high enough, but not her falling for him. Miranda, like a lot of people— most people in fact—responded to charm. Robert Thornton is an impressive figure in some ways, but eminently charmless. Anthony Avery is not a charmer, he's too much of a smoothie, and his essential toughness shows through. Guido di Montefalcone was charming. Morgan Grant is not. Gabriel Field has charm. So has Terence Fitzgerald.'

Dee is nothing if not quick on the uptake. 'So,' she stated, frowning, 'we now have the hypothesis that Miranda had a quickie fling with Gabriel, wanted to turn it into something more permanent, set up some sort of money-spinning plot with him, and Joyce, finding out and seeing history repeating itself, doctored the cocoa with the Major's capsules; she being the most likely person to know beforehand that they contained digitoxin which would be fatal on top of a normal or stepped-up dose of digitalis.'

'Yes. Or…'

'Joyce Bradley does not use the bathroom on our floor, though she may have popped into it once or twice. She had very limited access to Miranda's bedroom, and would have risked being seen going from one level to another. I always thought,' added Dee with seeming irrelevance, 'that that digital alarm was too obvious to be taken seriously as a cover-up, but now…'

'So what are we going to do about it all?'

'Oh,' declared my nearest and dearest airily, 'I'll think of something. Or you will.'

TERRY FITZGERALD was leaning over the bar, with a large and early pre-dinner drink in front of him, when I joined him and ordered a whisky and soda.

'Where's the little woman?' he demanded with a roguish twinkle.

'Oh—around somewhere. Exercising Bella, I think,' I said vaguely, and motioned to an alcove table, out of earshot of Betty. He followed me over, nursing his drink and looking a little puzzled.

'Collusion,' I stated succinctly.

'I beg your pardon?' Well might he gaze at me in that startled way. But before the expression of solicitous bewilderment (is the chap going off his rocker?) descended, I caught a brief wary flicker.

'You heard. You and Tony Avery know each other very well. You're both ambitious and unscrupulous. You're the ladies' man. You got onto Miranda's Mercury, somewhere in the course of seducing her, before, or after, and persuaded her to hand it over to you and Tony, telling her you were pretty sure it was a nineteenth century copy. But when that was verified by Tony's girlfriend, you had plans for disposing of it with maximum profit.'

Terry was deadpan. 'If so, no crime in that, is there?'

'I pass on that one, and on what exactly those plans were, except they involved fraud. To all intents and purposes Anthony and Jessica had a plan going that excluded you, and you were the innocent cat's-paw that had led them to the prize. But in fact it was to be a four-way split—you, Miranda, Anthony and Jessica. You suggested to Anthony that a three-way split would be much better, and that Miranda was obviously planning to ditch Thornton and might become a liability, and in any case was not to be trusted not to have a change of heart and ruin the whole thing. Since they had the Mercury and you were known to be on good terms with Miranda, but not suspected of carrying on more than a mild flirtation with her, the digital alarm alibi was set up to clear Anthony of suspicion. In fact, he was safely out of the way at his flat, as he stated.

'These were all very far-flung precautionary measures, because naturally your plan was to make it appear that Miranda had overdosed, under the influence of drink. You had already exaggerated her fondness for whisky to people. And certainly she seems to have been drinking before Robert Thornton turned up. His account indicates that, though he has not stated she was drunk. However, Miranda did not have enough digitalis tablets to ensure she died, so you were thrown back on the Major's capsules, which you had observed in the bathroom on your floor.'

'I can't believe this!' exclaimed Terry Fitzgerald, amazement effectively struggling with dawning anger on his features. 'The man's crazy! You've let your detective-story fantasies take you over. Sure, I ought to be sorry for you.'

I went on steadily, in the same calm monotone. 'In the scenario I envisage, you visited Miranda in her room, plied her with drink, slipped the powder you'd already removed from the capsules into her flask of cocoa while she was a bit woozy, possibly removing the flask to the bathroom where she could not see you and then surreptitiously returning it. You painted a rosy future together, with or without marriage as she chose, and playfully made her promise to drink up her cocoa like a good little girl. What she didn't tell you, probably suspecting you wouldn't like it, was that she'd not only given Robert Thornton the brush-off over the telephone, but he was due to arrive at The Grove to see her secretly.

'Miranda was feeling too woozy to come out of her room when the alarm went off, though she told Thornton subsequently she couldn't be bothered. She settled matters to her satisfaction with him and then followed your instructions and drank up the cocoa. The effect was pretty instant—a heart attack as she stumbled down after Thornton into the drawing-room. I doubt if she put two and two together in her last few seconds, but we'll never know, will we?'

'Of course this and the fact that Miranda hit her head on a table as she fell, making the whole thing appear like murder, and Dee's and my intervention, and Robert Thornton's presence and suspicions about the cocoa were things you had not foreseen. It must have been a dreadful shock when you stealthily made your way to Miranda's room in the early hours to find she was not there—dead or alive—but that the cup-top was off the flask and that the cocoa had been drunk. Even still, you didn't lose your cool, but washed up the flask carefully and returned to your room to await developments.'

Terry Fitzgerald took a large gulp of his drink, and raised his eyes skywards. Ironic amusement had replaced amazement and anger.

'You might as well go on, since I can't stop you,' he remarked in calm tones. 'You know, Vaughan, I begin to see why your stories are successful. Infinite imagination and an unlimited capacity for embroidery.'

'Thank you.' I continued. 'The impulsive Jessica, who is apt to do ill-considered and even stupid things, despite her obvious gifts, saw Thornton in his Mercedes en route to here—she'd been delayed and was pretty late herself. She put two and two together and decided to put pressure on Thornton to put money into Avery Antiques, possibly even opening another branch with Thornton as sleeping partner. In fact it was a sound business proposition, but since it was couched in terms of "If you do what we ask we won't tell on you", it was a particularly clumsy blackmail attempt, and Thornton naturally decided to reveal the events of that night to the police, even though this placed him in the light of suspect. This gave you more hope—Thornton's evidence, if true, made it clear Miranda's cocoa had been tampered with, but if he were guilty, either he had tampered with it himself, or the whole thing was a fabrication and the capsules' contents had been administered to Miranda some other way by Thornton.' I paused for a rest, while Fitzgerald continued to look ironic.

'If Thornton was cleared, I suppose there were other alternatives—the suggestion that Miranda had taken the capsules herself, in despair, after a quarrel with Thornton, and that he was trying to protect her name and his own. Or, as a last resort, throwing suspicion on someone else—perhaps the jealous Joyce Bradley. Maybe I misjudge you, and you wouldn't go as far as that, unless you were directly under suspicion yourself. But your mind is equally as fertile as my own, and full of self-protective devices.'

'This is all very fine,' returned Fitzgerald, in the conversational tone in which a tutor might discuss an unacceptable theory with a student in a seminar, 'but you haven't a shred of proof for your farrago of nonsense. And,' he added with a slow smile of triumph, 'if you think about it, I'm sure you'll realise that I'm not stupid enough to murder someone for the dubious profit of a three-way share in a fraudulent deal.'

'Excellent, Terry,' I commented. 'Your wits are

as sharp as I thought. You didn't make the mistake of referring to the passing-off of the copy as a real Cellini Mercury, which would have proved your knowledge of the plan and connivance in it. No, you stuck to the words I used. Very clever. And, oh, yes, I agree with you. Good as the plot sounds, with Jessica in on it with her connections and reputation as a Renaissance expert, it still posed dangers. Not least of them the arrogant and indiscreet Miss Downes herself. Avery might have done it, but not you. On the other hand, Avery believed you would do it, and would have backed you up out of loyalty as well as self-interest. Naturally both of you were counting on Miranda's death being taken as suicide or fatal accident while the balance of her mind was temporarily affected by drink or depression or whatever. But, to return to the point you raised, there was a bigger prize in sight, wasn't there?'

I could see by the quick movement of the head, the flicker of the eyelids and the slight flare of the nostrils, that I had him.

'There were two Cellini Mercuries, weren't there? But no one saw the other one—the real one. Not even you or Miranda herself. Because Guido sent a message with the Santagram, didn't he, which you made sure was destroyed. Burnt in an ashtray, probably, or flushed down the loo. And that message told Miranda the copy Mercury was to fool would-be burglars, etc and the real thing had already been deposited in a very respectable and very long-founded bank in the city of London. So you and Miranda were conning Anthony and Jessica into thinking she really believed at first that the Mercury in her possession was the Renaissance one, and that when she found out it wasn't she'd be so furious and feel so cheated that she'd be all too willing to join the swindle plot. So—you got in for a hefty cut of that, if it came off. And meanwhile there was the real thing waiting to be collected.'

'What was in your favour was the fact that in twentieth century England it is hardly believable that a man would give a priceless gift like this to a girl, however beautiful, especially if she was not engaged to him and had other suitors as well. But Guido di Montefalcone is an extraordinary mixture, by all accounts—part playboy, part Don Quixote. Very concerned with the concept of honour, and one for the big extravagant gesture—the bigger and more extravagant the better. True, he'll bankrupt the family if he goes on like this, but no doubt the other members of it will act as some kind of re-straining influence. And who knows how intense the effect that Miranda, a figure straight from the canvas of a Botticelli painting, may have had on him? I think you were banking on the fact that whereas even Guido might have been motivated to demand the Cellini back if Miranda married Robert Thornton, if she were dead he would be more likely to let matters rest; certainly until the family's grief had died down, and then perhaps offer to buy it back at a generous sum. He might *even* let it go altogether. But, of course, you charmed Miranda into scuppering her chances with Thornton, then cold-bloodedly disposed of her. Do you mind?' I indicated my empty glass and sauntered over to the bar to get a refill, just as the Major came in.

'Ah, Major, will you join us? And may I congratulate you on your sense of timing.'

Hemmed in on one side by me and on the other by Major Gardner, Fitzgerald's resemblance to a creature at bay increased. There were beads of sweat on his forehead and above his upper lip now.

'The Major is a JP, which you knew. He began to worry about the promissory note, written and signed by Miranda in his presence and signed as a witness by him, authorising you to remove the wrapped object deposited for her in the vaults in Lombard Street. Failing a solicitor on the premises, the Major was the best you could find to give credibility to Miranda's note. When he asked you about it, after Miranda's death, you managed to pass the matter off, telling him the arrangement you'd had with Miranda (which you didn't specify) was no longer operative, and you had destroyed the note. Of course, even if the Major had decided to investigate and take the matter up with the bank later, you would have collected the statuette and real provenance, and would have been safely out of the country. You counted on the Major's trust in human nature, believing what you said, and leaving the matter. But Major Gardner is a wilier old bird than you thought, isn't that right, Major, and when I started questioning him as to what he knew about you, he came out with the story, which he would probably have told the police in the next few days, anyway.'

'You were too greedy, young man, that was your trouble,' Major Gardner said sorrowfully. 'And greed begets evil and still more greed.'

'Save me the preaching,' Fitzgerald snarled contemptuously. Mean and dangerous as he looked now, I almost felt sorry for him, as I played the final card.

'I've been beavering away today, hoping to gather some definite evidence. You see, Miranda was entitled to life; romantic and generous Guido is entitled to his family heirloom back. Moreover, you were directly responsible in shattering Robert Thornton's image of Miranda and in double-crossing your partner. I don't know whether this will stand up in court or not, but Betty Brewer was up early the morning of Boxing Day, as she couldn't sleep. She didn't go to the drawing-room, or she'd have found Miranda's body long before my wife did. But at about 5.30 she was doing some clearing out in the upstairs rooms—the ones that aren't normally in use. Looking down from the windows you can see directly onto the rooms round the corner from us on our corridor. At least, you don't look directly onto the main windows in room thirteen, Miranda's room, but you do overlook the bathroom window—which was open, and where you were carefully washing and drying out a flask. Betty has been too upset to think straight, and she returned to bed after doing her tidying. I doubt if she'd ever have thought of it again if the matter of the flask hadn't become central—and if I hadn't been asking around about you. But then, again, we'll never know, will we? I'm afraid you've lost your high-stakes game, Terry.'

FOURTEEN

The End

Dee

I DON'T KNOW how we got away from The Grove, but in due course we managed it. Barry even managed to polish off the last section of *Framed Murder* before we departed, and it came out at Easter, to coincide with the third reprint of one of the earlier books. I never thought I'd be panting to return to the crowded suburbs, but I was. The rolling downs and picturesque oasthouses are all very well, but somehow our cosy Christmas holiday had turned into more of a stretch penned up in durance vile.

'At least,' I remarked to Barry when we were back on our home turf, 'you solved the murder. Ken Graves should be undyingly grateful to you— he hardly did a thing; you did it all.'

'Well, he was called in late, and we did have the advantage of knowing the terrain, plus the personnel. Anyway, Dee, you certainly did your bit, down at Avery Antiques—I sort of sat around like Sherlock Holmes, just working it out.'

'Very cleverly, too.'

'Oh, I don't know,' Barry demurred modestly. 'What the Major told me made it all fall into place. Before that, I wasn't too sure it *was* Terry Fitzgerald. My re-creation of his motives and actions involved a lot of guesswork—inspired perhaps, but as he pointed out, likely to be taken as the meanderings of an over-imaginative detective story writer. Also, Terry seemed so damned likeable and harmless. You always stress motive, Dee, and once I suspected about the second, genuine Cellini, it made me convinced. His big mistake was approaching Major Gardner, but I suppose he was afraid the bank officials wouldn't give up the package and a JP's signature might establish his bona fides.'

'Terry fell for your story about Betty and her sudden cleaning mania.'

Barry grimaced wryly. 'Yes, because I sprang it on him at the moment when he was thoroughly shaken. He admitted washing out the flask, but even then he managed to think up a plausible enough explanation. Anyway, he denied it all later, so it didn't work after all. Like my idea of planting the tape at Redditch Grange. That wasn't exactly the scoop of the century either.'

I gave him a hug. 'Never mind, darling, you do try. And sometimes you succeed. Brilliantly.'

'Logical deduction and inspired guesswork,' Barry murmured, but he looked gratified all the same. 'The worst part is,' he added with a sigh, 'I feel awful having Fitzgerald hauled in. Like a copper's nark.'

'Nonsense,' I said firmly. 'The way he was developing, he'd probably have gone on to rob the Vatican and poison the Pope. And though Miranda turns out to have been a thoroughly nasty little two-timing bitch with criminal instincts of her own, on top of being a pampered spoilt brat—well, lots of people cared about her. And she was so terribly young to die. Anyway,' I pointed out, 'I'm sure all investigators feel like that. Think of the *nice* things.'

'What nice things?'

'Well, poor Robin and Betty being able to get back to normal. And the Major feeling he's acquired some purpose in life and joining that organisation for the Preservation of Whatever-it-is. And my lovely jade horse. And finishing your book in spite of all the alarums and excursions.'

So—life went on as usual, with me back at the agency and Barry back at the Tech. Till we were called as witnesses at the trial. The jury took a long time over their verdict, but eventually Terence Fitzgerald was acquitted—insufficient evidence against him. Since Anthony Avery and Jessica Downes had also got off on charges of aiding and abetting, and since no fraud had as yet been perpetrated by them, that was that.

Avery Antiques continued to prosper, minus the partnership of Terry Fitzgerald, who emigrated to America, I believe, after a period going to ground. I felt rather relieved he wasn't in the country—who knows, he might have conducted a hate campaign against Barry, as being instrumental in his arrest. Both of us felt the gravest doubts about Fitzgerald becoming a model citizen. I imagine he'd find plenty of opportunities for palming off dubious antique works—but I don't suppose we'll ever know anything of his subsequent life.

Bella missed Fifi and Ajax for a while, but eventually realised that holiday friends tend to disappear, sad though it is. We praised The Grove to various people, but next Christmas I think we'll stay firmly at home. Or perhaps a nice, healthy skiing holiday…

Talking of nice things, Barry remarked casually one day, 'I hope Anthony and Jessica never got their mitts on the copy Mercury.'

'They didn't.' I smiled smugly.

'How do you know?'

'Ha-ha.'

'I don't believe you do know.'

'Oh, yes I do.'

'Oh no you don't.'

We have been known to keep up this kind of

childish exchange for five minutes at a time, but this time I spiked his guns by revealing, 'I do, because I took it on myself to visit Morgan Grant at his studio flat one day and I advised him to buy Mercury from Miranda's family, as a keepsake. And they ended up *giving* it to him!'

'Cor! They don't sound much like Miranda!'

'Well, she'd probably have turned out quite nice if she hadn't been so beautiful. Morgan says they're perfectly normal, and they felt sorry for him for having been keen on *La Primavera* for so long and having to go through the trauma of knowing she was murdered.'

'I should have imagined it was more of a trauma for them!'

'Well, of course, but they've got four other children, scattered around, all much older than Miranda, and numerous grandchildren. Miranda was their Benjamin, so to speak, but she'd cut herself off quite a bit, and I think they knew what she was like. Still awful for them, of course, but not as awful as if she were the only one. I got all this from Morgan,' I explained. 'What about the original Mercury, though? Now you're the one who'd know about that, Barry.'

'Via Ken Graves. Yes. Well, you will be relieved to hear that it's back in The Palazzo in Umbria, restored to the di Montefalcones, proof of provenance and all.'

'Good. Castello.'

'Pardon?'

'Castle, not palace.'

'Well, these places are all much the same.'

I didn't argue the point, and instead I said, 'Joyce Bradley wrote to me the other day.'

'Really? Has she split up with young Gabe yet?'

'On the contrary. He inherited rather a lot of money from an aunt; or rather, it was a rambling mausoleum of a property, which Gabriel put up for sale and with the proceeds bought the flat above Joyce's and the next-door semi, and they're running the whole caboodle as bedsits for students. They're getting married at Easter and guess where they're spending their honeymoon?'

'Not The Grove!'

'No, of course not! Florence.'

'Hmm. I think,' said Barry in heartfelt tones, 'if we visit that city again in the next decade, I shall avoid all paintings by Botticelli.'

'And all works of any kind whatsoever by Cellini.'

'Perhaps,' suggested Barry, looking at the jade horse, 'we'll go to China and get into Ming and Sung and Tang.'

'Too expensive, alas. But how about Peking Duck for dinner—or chop suey takeaway?'

Bella pricked up her ears at the word 'dinner'.

'And Chunky Morsels with fried rice for Bella.'

'Woof,' agreed Bella.

SKYE KATHLEEN MOODY

BLUE POPPY

A VENUS DIAMOND MYSTERY

The butterfly collector's deathbed is a carpet of fresh grass and wildflowers. He's clutching a bunch of blue poppies, cultivated on an ecological preserve by Avalon, makers of the exclusive Blue Poppy perfume.

It doesn't take Fish and Wildlife Agent Venus Diamond long to discover that the area's fragile ecosystem has been exploited by more than murder.

Available December 1998, where books are sold.

Look us up on-line at: http://www.romance.net   WSKM293